Once you know what you're doing, composting is surprisingly easy—and incredibly effective. And it helps save the earth while saving you money.

This guide will tell you . . .   05

- ❋ how moisture and air circulation affect your compost
- ❋ which ingredients are safe to include in the pile
- ❋ how to keep pests at bay
- ❋ how to use compost for starting seeds and transplants
- ❋ how to buy a bin . . . or build your own and much more!

THE COMPLETE BOOK OF COMPOST

The Complete

Book of Compost

by Robert Francis

becker & mayer!
BOOKS

B

BERKLEY BOOKS, NEW YORK

THE COMPLETE BOOK OF COMPOST

A Berkley Book / published by arrangement with the
author

PRINTING HISTORY
Berkley edition / April 1998

The Penguin Putnam Inc. World Wide Web site address is
http://www.penguinputnam.com

ISBN: 0-425-16264-8

BERKLEY®
Berkley Books are published by The Berkley Publishing Group,
a member of
Penguin Putnam Inc., 200 Madison Avenue, New York, New York 10016.
BERKLEY and the "B" design are trademarks belonging to
Berkley Publishing Corporation.

PRINTED IN THE UNITED STATES OF AMERICA

10 9 8 7 6 5 4 3 2 1

This book is dedicated to my grandparents,

Kate and Harry,

who taught me the true meaning of generosity.

CONTENTS

The
Complete
Book of
Compost

WHAT IS COMPOST

AND

WHY SHOULD YOU MAKE IT?

*H*ERE'S AN OLD FAVORITE RECIPE FOR making compost: "Mix two parts fall leaves with one part grass clippings. Add a generous amount of kitchen scraps and a few billion common microorganisms. Moisten and put aside for a few months. Turn as needed."

Is composting really that easy? Emphatically, yes! Compost is embarrassingly easy to make and almost impossible to botch. When plants die, they naturally decompose and return to the soil. When we heap them up and compost them, we're just speeding up nature's decay cycle a little. And our end result is a sweet-smelling crumbly soil that's the finest organic fertilizer on earth.

Grab a handful of finished compost. It's hard to believe that this rich brown humus was once pine needles from your front yard, dandelions pulled in May, watermelon rinds from a summer picnic, and a few Earl Grey tea bags from Aunt Molly's last visit. In just a few months these worthless discards have been magically recycled into a disease-fighting, soil-building plant food that both your tomatoes and tulips will love.

And plants aren't the only lovers of compost. Thrifty homeowners love making compost for the money it saves them in gardening supplies. Why should we toss out all our grass clippings and fall leaves only to turn around and buy expensive sacks of topsoil and peat moss at the garden center? Municipalities across the nation also have a love affair with compost. They know that up to half of the stuff people drag to their curbs each week could instead be recycled in their own backyard piles. When communities compost, the savings in trash-hauling costs and landfill fees are enormous.

Yet, home composting has a definite image problem. We fear we'll create a slimy heap of garbage and attract vermin to our homes. Or that the neighbors will complain of the smell. Or that the board of health will come knocking at the door. But truth be told, if you follow the few simple rules of thumb outlined here, your compost pile will be a well-mannered, unobtrusive addition to your home landscape. There's a way of composting that suits anyone's needs and desires. You can start a casual heap near your woodlot, or you can buy a smart-looking bin designed to blend in with the bushes. You can build an elegant three-bin system with a shingled roof, or you can simply keep a worm box on your porch or balcony. You can compost in a barrel, a box, a bin, or a bag.

Whether you're a suburban lawn baron, an urban tree hugger, or a rural recycler, there's no excuse not to compost. Everything you need to know is here in this small book. And just as we've all learned how fast and easy it is to separate our glass bottles and aluminum cans for the recycling bins, we can learn and practice the humble art of composting.

WHAT'S SO GOOD ABOUT COMPOST ANYWAY?

Compost is every gardener's best friend. Here are some of its finer qualities:

※ Compost's crumbly, fibrous nature fluffs up clay soils and helps sandy soils hold water.

※ Compost provides a slow, even release of plant nutrients and stimulates root growth.

※ Compost suppresses soil-borne plant diseases.

⚡ Compost prevents erosion of our fast-depleting topsoil.

※ Compost recycles tons of yard wastes.

Other less tangible rewards are also bestowed on composters. There's the spiritual reward of becoming an active participant in the ageless miracle of decay and rebirth. And there's the educational bonus of experiencing firsthand the science of soil-building in your own backyard. And perhaps best of all, there's the fun that you and your family will have watching your garbage turn to gold. And by the simple act of starting a pile today, you'll become a better gardener, a better citizen, and perhaps a better human being all at once.

Happy composting!

A Closer Look Inside the Pile

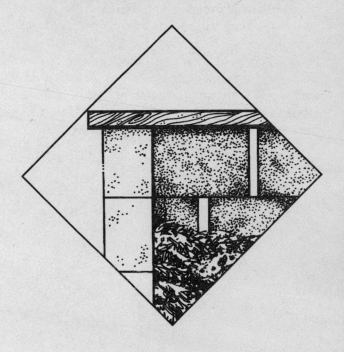

THE CYCLE OF LIFE

O N THIS PLANET, DECAY IS A NATURAL and essential part of the cycle of life and death—and be glad it is, or we'd all be up to our eyeballs in dead dinosaurs and day-old doughnuts. In every forest, grassland, jungle, and garden, plants and animals die, fall to the ground, and decay. In time their stems, feathers, leaves, and bones are slowly dismantled by the millions of small organisms living in the soil. Eventually these plant and animal parts become indistinguishable from the earth around them— their complex structures have disappeared completely into the chocolaty brown crumbly matter that covers the forest floor.

Much of what was once alive is now dissolved into proteins, enzymes, and minerals—valuable nutrients reduced to simple molecular forms and ready to be reabsorbed by the next generation of growing plants. If you pick up a handful of this rich, fertile loam and examine it closely, you might still see small bits of twigs or feathers. These are the slower-decaying pieces of dead plants and animals. They, too, will eventually be reduced to simple molecules, but in the meantime they keep the soil light and fluffy and allow the tender young roots of new plants to better penetrate the soil and take advantage of those nutritious molecules. Mother Nature, the greatest recycler of all, has done it again. She's made a miracle substance called humus.

The creation of humus is our goal when we start composting. In fact, "compost" is just another word for "homemade humus," and our compost piles are simply small working models of Mother Nature's forest floor. We feed our piles the dead plant matter from our yards and kitchens and wait until it is transformed into something useful—compost—which we'll turn around and use to feed our new rosebushes and radish rows.

The only difference between our little decay factories and Mother Nature's great big forests is that we usually like to organize and hasten the decomposition process. Why? Several reasons: First of all, making compost faster creates heat, which helps destroy plant diseases and weed seeds that may be lurking in our pile. Also, faster decomposition means we can process more raw ingredients from our yards and kitchens. And finally, we're just not as patient as Mother Nature, are we?

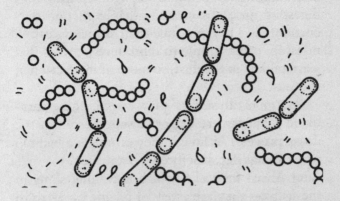

But who is ultimately responsible for all this decay work, anyway? Well, we can certainly see the earthworms and all their wiggly associates creeping about our compost. These *macroorganisms*—animals we can see—are on the payroll for sure, but it's the even tinier unseen *microorganisms*—bacteria, fungi, and yeasts—that do the lion's share of decomposition. These microorganisms are present everywhere and in great numbers—bunches of them are present on your hands and this book right now—ready to find something dead to decompose. And once they find that dead thing, they feed on it with great gusto, ripping into old banana peels or beech tree leaves, reducing them to smaller bits, and releasing their nutrients for another generation of plants. Far from being fussy eaters, these microorganisms produce enzymes capable of digesting just about any organic matter they encounter. They continue their voracious eating nonstop, pausing only to reproduce (at rates that leave rabbits in the dust) so more of them can join the feast.

As opportunistic as they sound, these insatiable small fry are truly the superheroes of the decay process. Although they often get a bad rap when things decay before we want them to—like Aunt Alice's fruitcake, which is turning slimy in the fridge—they are essential for life on earth to continue. And indeed, some microorganisms have been harnessed to produce products we enjoy, such as wine, yogurt, blue cheese, and beer. So don't bad-mouth all the bacteria before you know the score. Make friends with some of them instead, and get them to work for you in your compost pile.

PUTTING OUT THE WEE WELCOME MAT

When we start a batch of compost, our goal is to create an ideal environment for our diminutive decomposers where they'll eat, drink, hang out, and multiply. If you treat your microbial guests well, they'll work hard for you. In a nutshell, here's what they need:

A BALANCED DIET. An ideal bacterial buffet would include some nice dried brown things like straw or fall leaves, mixed in well with a smaller amount of fresh, juicy green things like grass

clippings or kitchen scraps. Our small friends get their energy from the carbon in brown things, much as we get our energy from carbohydrates. And, just like us, they need protein, which they find in nitrogen-rich green things. Of course they prefer the food to be chopped, ground, shredded, or torn into smaller pieces so they can stuff their tiny mouths more easily.

SOME FRESH AIR.   The mightiest of the mini-microbes are fresh air fiends. These *aerobic* organisms (imagine them in tiny Reeboks) are the quickest decomposers around, and they'll keep on going as long as they have enough air to breathe. They also give off heat as a by-product, which helps destroy weed seeds and disease organisms in the compost pile. If they don't get enough air, however, they'll pack it up and leave the rest of the job to their slouchy cousins, the *anaerobic* microbes. These guys can do the dirty work of decomposition without oxygen, but they don't produce heat, they don't work fast, and they often smell bad. So to keep our athletic friends in the majority, we must find ways to supply them with plenty of air.

A DRINK OF WATER.   Like all living things, our tiny tenants need water to keep working hard. If the pile gets too dry, the mini-microbes will go into hibernation and your lovely compost pile will sit and mummify. But too much water will drown out the aerobic bacteria you want to cultivate, and the smelly anaerobic bacteria will move in. Make your beneficial bacteria happy by keeping the pile moist but not sopping wet.

A WARM BED.   One by-product of a huge bacterial buffet is heat. All that furious feeding can raise the temperature in the center of a compost pile to 170° F. That's hot enough to cook an egg! But instead of cooking breakfast on a raging compost pile, we'd much rather cook any weed seeds or *plant pathogens* (harmful microorganisms that attack living plants) which might be lurking about. The high heat also dramatically speeds up the entire decomposition process so we get better quality compost and we get it faster. To turn our piles on high, we must build them up to a certain minimum size or all the heat they generate will be dissipated before it does any good.

A ROTTIN' TOUR THROUGH AN IDEAL PILE

Now that we know what it takes to make compost happen, let's take a worm's-eye tour through an ideal pile. Let's assume we've collected the right ingredients in the right proportions and added the right amount of moisture. We've built the pile up to the right size and provided adequate air circulation to allow the aerobic bacteria to breathe.

At first, some larger macroorganisms begin to investigate the pile. Red worms are seen diving in and out of the kitchen scraps. Beetles and ants

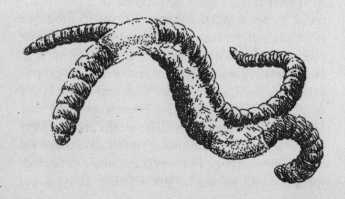

roam about selecting tasty morsels. But most important, certain bacteria that are active at cooler temperatures begin to eat and reproduce. These are known as *psychrophiles*. As they begin to feed on the waste materials, their tiny sweaty bodies generate heat, and the pile begins to warm up. The temperature rises steadily as these bacteria eat and eat and eat and reproduce. Eventually the psychrophiles become overheated and enter a nonactive dormant stage as a different group of bacteria—the *mesophiles*—kick in. They're better suited to this warmer environment, and they also generate heat as they eat. When the pile reaches about 120°F., the mesophiles throw in the towel and give their hotheaded brothers, the *thermophiles*, a chance to chow down. These bacteria thrive in the heated interior of the pile and continue to consume the raw leaves, twigs, and scraps at a quicker pace.

The pile keeps getting hotter—it may reach a temperature of 160° F. to 170° F., and steam may appear when you stir the compost. The worms and other insects have retreated to the cooler bottom and edges of the pile to wait this thing out. The intense heat generated by thermophilic bacterial activity begins to kill any weed seeds that may have ended up in your pile. Disease organisms from unhealthy plants are also destroyed by the high temperatures.

The pile shrinks and compacts as the raw ingredients are converted into simpler materials. A good turning of the pile at this point will replenish oxygen to the aerobic bacteria and help get the outer materials into the center of the hot pile where they rot more quickly. You may also need to moisten the pile a little if it has become too dry.

The voracious thermophiles continue to feed until the pile gets too hot even for them or until they run out of food. Once they stop, the pile begins to cool down, and the mesophiles, psychrophiles, worms, and insects come back out of the woodwork to finish off the leftovers. When the pile has reached ambient temperature again, we're left with beautiful bucketfuls of sweet-smelling crumbly humus.

How long the process takes from raw materials to finished compost depends on many factors. A pile started with chunky ingredients that isn't turned or watered may take years to decompose. On the other hand, a tumbler unit filled with the correct proportions of shredded leaves and grass clippings and a little manure can often be made into humus in fourteen days. Once you know how composting works, you can decide how fast or slow you want your pile to rot.

Since most people don't have the time and

patience to organize and monitor an ideal pile, their compost may not reach the thermophilic hot stage. Your pile may be too small, or the ingredient ratio may be off, or the weather may be too cold for it to get to the red-hot temperature of the ideal pile described above. But that's not a cause for worry. It just means that your compost will take a little longer to finish. And if you make an effort to keep out seedy weeds and diseased plants to begin with, you'll still finish with a fine homemade compost that is excellent for all your gardening needs.

OTHER DECOMPOSERS

Microorganisms aren't the only creatures that live in your compost bin. Macroorganisms, animals big enough to see without a microscope, are also running around munching on dead plant material, microorganisms, and, more often than not, each other. Beetles eat fungal spores, flatworms eat earthworms, ants eat just about anything. (As Woody Allen once said of the natural world "It's really like one big restaurant, isn't it?") So don't be surprised when you see these creepy crawlies scurrying about your bin. They belong there too. Here's a brief field guide to these more visible players:

EARTHWORMS. Earthworms spend their lives eating soil and other organic matter. They leave behind castings—one of the richest, most nutritive parts of compost. Earthworms are such wonderful decomposers that many people compost exclusively with them (see Chapter 11.) They are nature's finest tunnelers, continually churning and turning the soil, aerating and loosening, creating tunnels that allow plant roots to penetrate deeper.

SOW BUGS. Also known as pill bugs, sow bugs resemble little armadillos, with their segmented bodies. They eat decaying plant matter and roll up into a tiny ball when threatened.

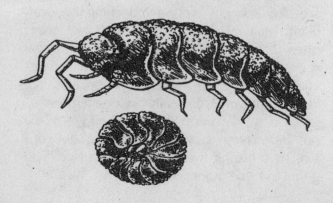

SLUGS. These slimy, amorphous creatures, which move quite slowly, are mollusks that lack a shell. They dine on plant material, both living and dead, so while they may be beneficial in your pile, you don't want to see them in your garden beds.

SNAILS. Unmistakable in their shells, snails are also mollusks that move about with a thick, retractable foot. They eat what slugs eat and are more common in the western parts of the country. Again, these are creatures not welcome in a garden.

BEETLES. Many beetles make a compost pile their home. Some eat the tiny spores of micro-

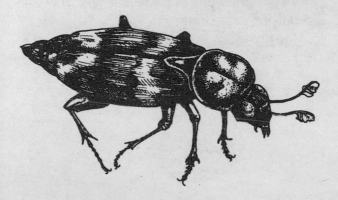

scopic fungi while others eat a variety of insects. The black rove beetle preys on snails and slugs, making many gardeners happy.

ANTS.   Ants are everywhere and eat a wide variety of materials, including seeds, kitchen scraps, fungi, and other insects. Their presence may be beneficial, as their tireless tunneling moves nutrients about in the bin and creates some air circulation.

FLIES.   Fruit flies, houseflies, gnats, and other flies may appear at times buzzing about the top of your pile, especially if you've just added a quantity of kitchen scraps. Even though they help with decomposition, flies can be annoying. Keep a bag or barrel of dried leaves or grass clippings to the side and use them to cover your daily additions of kitchen scraps. This will keep flying insects away.

COMPOSTING WITH STYLE

*E*VERY COMPOST PILE IS AS UNIQUE AS the gardener who got it started and usually reflects that individual's personality. Some people compost for environmental reasons only; they simply want to reduce the trash stream that emanates from their home and yard. Market gardeners and farmers make compost because they need as much of it as possible to enrich their topsoil and improve crop production. Still other people compost to avoid expensive trash-hauling fees. Whatever your reasons are for starting a compost pile, you'll find a method here that will fit your lifestyle and your yard.

To get you started, here are a select set of compost strategies. All of them work, and all of them can be adapted to your needs, your schedule, and the raw ingredients you have access to in and around your home. Feel free to mix and match techniques, and you'll be on your way to a personal style of composting.

The Passive Pile-Up

The way most people compost: passively. To do this, you build or buy a simple bin, stick it in the corner of your yard, and add grass clippings and autumn leaves. Moisten the pile with a hose if it gets too dry, but don't turn it. If you're not quite that lazy and want to keep your trash cans lighter and fresher smelling, start adding your watermelon rinds, corncobs, potato peelings, and other kitchen scraps to the pile. The bin may get too full on occasion, but the pile will shrink within a short period of time as the materials compress and decompose. Wait a year or two before checking the bottom of the bin for finished compost. When it's ready, disassemble the bin or open the little trapdoors toward the bottom of many of the manufactured units. Shovel the finished compost into buckets or a cart, and add it to your garden beds. Some of the stuff toward the top of the pile is still not decomposed, collect it back into the bin to finish by next year.

Composting in Bed

Do you have a big garden and a bad back? Then make your compost right where you'll use it. Start by filling up a simple bin right on top of an unused garden bed. You won't be able to plant there this year, but when that batch of compost is ready, you can simply remove the bin and let all that beautiful black gold spill over the ground for next season's crop. Then start a new bin on a different bed. Keep moving the location until you've covered the entire garden.

Underground Compost

Known as *sheet*, *pit*, or *trench composting*, this is a way of making compost right where you need it most—in the garden soil. You simply dig a hole or trench at least a foot deep and dump in your ingredients. Cover it up with a few inches of soil and then continue adding more materials and covering them with soil. You can also spread your organic ingredients over a bed and with a rototiller set at maximum depth or with a hand spade, if the bed is small, work them into the soil. Either way, the material will decompose in place, and when it's done, you won't have to haul it to some other part of the yard. This is a slow anaerobic (without air) process, but there will be no odors as long as the material is covered up. Good ingredients to use in sheet composting are grass clippings, leaves, and manure. Food scraps work fine, but they may attract four-footed animals to your garden. As with all composting, smaller pieces make for faster compost.

This technique is best suited for an area in the garden where you won't be planting this year, as the underground rotting can temporarily reduce the available nitrogen in the soil. If there are too many brown (high-carbon) ingredients, the nitrogen in the soil will become tied up temporarily and unavailable to hungry plant roots. If you want to plant in these high-carbon areas immediately, add a high nitrogen material like manure, blood meal, or cottonseed meal to keep the soil in balance. Set up a rotation plan for your garden so that some beds are planted while others are being filled with raw materials.

Red-Hot Compost

Do you want fast and furiously steaming heaps? Here's a pile style so hot it will destroy most weed seeds and other pathogens yet still yield crumbly compost in as little as fourteen days. To build such a furnace, you must construct it all at once, paying careful attention to the balance of carbon (browns) and nitrogen (greens) as well as moisture content.

Here's one recipe: Start with a base of straw and add a thin layer (less than 3 inches) of well-chopped greens (such as grass clippings, seaweed, and kitchen scraps), followed by a thin layer of browns (such as rotting straw or shredded leaves), followed by a thin layer of garden soil or compost to inoculate the pile. Continue adding layers and periodically moisten the pile as it is built. After a few days the temperature will soar due to the microbial activity. You can even buy a compost thermometer to check this rise if you like. Once the temperature starts to drop, turn the pile thoroughly to aerate and mix the outer ingredients with the inner ones. Wait for the pile to reheat and turn it again. Repeat until the pile cools and you should have beautiful compost ready for the garden. Tumbler-type composters are great for this, as they can be turned easily.

Cosmic Composting

Practitioners of *biodynamic farming* build their compost piles in very special ways. They follow a system of agriculture first outlined by the Austrian philosopher Rudolf Steiner (1861–1925), who continually searched for the common threads that united all living processes. Very popular in Europe, biodynamicists use many traditional organic gardening methods, but also follow very specific techniques—such as coordinating their activities to the phases of the moon—to ensure that their crops are in sync with the cosmos.

Start a biodynamic compost pile by digging a shallow pit 5 to 10 inches deep and then covering it with a thin layer of manure or finished compost. Then you add your ingredients in layers no thicker than 2 inches, followed by a covering of soil. The pile starts as a 12- to 15-foot-wide structure tapering to 6 feet wide at its maximum height (5 or 6 feet).

Next, add a special compost activator—made from a secret combination of wild plants and available only through certified biodynamic sources—to the pile. You then cover the pile with hay or leaves and let it sit for three to five months before turning. For more information regarding the biodynamic method, write to the Farming and Gardening Association, P. O. Box 550, Kimberton, PA 19442, 800-516-7797.

The Pileless Pile

Back in the 1950s, Ruth Stout, a crusty New Englander, popularized a no-work method of gardening that is still used today. Ruth did not believe in spending hour after hour cultivating, hoeing, weeding, and fertilizing her vegetables. She avoided such dreary tasks by using a very thick layer of mulch that covered her entire garden. Instead of composting her grass clippings, leaves, and other yard waste, she piled them evenly over her beds, pulling the material back only when she wanted to plant seeds or drop in a transplant. The thick mulch prevented any weeds from growing and kept the soil moist. While the mulch was never thick enough to heat up, as it would in a compost pile, it did decompose slowly over the years, returning nutrients to the soil.

If you decide to mulch with your raw materials, keep an eye out for moles, mice, and slugs. They enjoy a nice thick mulch as much as Ruth did.

The Leaf-Me-Alone Pile

If autumn leaves are the only crop your backyard produces, consider making leaf-only piles. Simply stack the leaves in a wire bin or in a less windy corner of your yard, wet them thoroughly, and wait a few years. Eventually they will rot into a dark, crumbly, water-absorbent material known as leaf mold. While not as nutritious as compost, leaf mold makes a wonderful mulch for use around your garden transplants, and it can be worked into any soil that needs improvement. Of course, shredding and turning the leaves will speed up the process considerably.

The Three-Bin Pile-Up

If you have a big yard, you might consider buying or building a multi-bin composting setup. Two bins are good, but three are great. Having three bins means that you can build a pile and then leave it to rot without slowing it down with additional ingredients. Fresh materials can then go toward a new pile in the empty bin next door. And when it comes time to turn the piles, you can easily fork them right over into the empty third bin.

The Micro Compost Pile

If you're really stuck for space, consider composting in a bucket. Find a clean 5-gallon plastic bucket and throw a little peat moss or sawdust in the bottom. Add kitchen scraps and cover them with additional peat or sawdust. Continue adding layers and stir, poke, or prod with a garden hand tool to mix things up. If the pile gets too wet, it may start to smell and you may need to add additional peat or sawdust. Once the bucket is filled, you can start another while the first one cooks. In a few months the compost should be ready to use.

HOW TO MAKE
COMPOST

MAKING COMPOST IS NOT A COMPLI-cated undertaking. Any pile of dead plant material will eventually rot all by itself. But if you want a compost pile that's efficient and well behaved, you're best off following the few basic rules outlined in this chapter.

CONTAINERS

Our primitive gardening ancestors—*Homo compostus*—didn't bother much with containers when they made compost. They just heaped up piles of the right ingredients, added water, and occasionally turned a pile when they became bored chasing butterflies or other primitive gardeners. This is how farmers around the world have made compost for centuries, and it's a perfectly fine way of rotting your wastes into a useful product. An unenclosed compost pile is easy to turn, easy to move, and costs nothing to set up.

But open stacks of yard waste won't fit into most backyard landscapes. Unencumbered heaps of garden refuse and grass clippings look messy

and will likely offend your neighbors. And if you include kitchen scraps in your mix, you might attract rodents or dogs or cats that could tear apart and scatter the raw materials. So most people choose to compost in a neater fashion by using one of two types of containers: bins or tumblers.

Compost Bins

Bins are the most common type of compost container. A compost bin is simply a box constructed of plastic, metal, wood, or stone with holes or slots in the sides to provide air circulation. It may or may not have a lid to keep out pests and to control excess rainfall and moisture evaporation. Bins of all sorts and sizes are man-

ufactured by dozens of companies, but you can easily build one out of scrap bits of wood, wire, and whatever else is on hand, using one of the plans outlined in the following chapter. When bin-made compost is ready, you usually remove the finished product by disassembling the bin. Some commercial bins have small trapdoors at the base so you can remove finished compost from the bottom of the pile without fussing with the unfinished upper sections.

Compost-makers with enough yard space might consider buying more than one bin or build a multi-bin unit. Having extra bins will allow you to start a new heap while an earlier pile is cooking away. You can also fork a rotting pile over into an empty bin, effectively mixing, aerating and restacking the ingredients all at once.

Compost Tumblers

Tumbler-type composters are essentially bins with tight-fitting lids that can be rotated by hand for maximum aeration and blending of ingredients. They are generally more expensive to buy and fairly difficult to build, but if used properly, they can produce buckets of compost in a wink. The thorough turnings ensure adequate air circulation and a good mixing of ingredients to accelerate decomposition. Most tumbler units sit on a sturdy metal frame and spin on their sides; others turn head over heels. There are also newer types that resemble large balls that can be pushed around the yard by your hyperactive children.

Tumblers are generally a little smaller than bins, because compost is heavy stuff. And although you still have to lift the ingredients into the unit, you can let the finished compost pour out into a cart or wagon when it's ready—a nice plus for folks with weak backs.

LOCATION

When selecting a site for your future pile, start by looking for a level, well-drained area. If you plan to add kitchen scraps, keep it closer to the back door so you won't have to shovel a path all the way to the back fence after every snowfall. Think also of where you normally empty the grass-catcher bag during your summer mowings. If you plan to augment your pile with bags of leaves from your neighbors' yards or manure from local stables (don't laugh, serious composters cruise for this stuff), site your pile nearer the driveway. And don't keep the pile under a downspout or gutter or anyplace where excessive water will collect when it rains.

The climate will also determine where your pile should go. In cooler latitudes, keep the heap in a sunny spot to trap that extra solar heat. In warmer, drier climes, shelter the pile in a shadier spot so it doesn't dry out too quickly. Look for a sheltered spot in northern areas to protect your pile from freezing cold winds; they could slow down the decay process, and they might blow off the lid, if you have one.

Unless rats and mice become a significant problem (and they usually won't), try to build your pile on top of the soil or lawn rather than on a concrete patio or asphalt driveway. By keeping the pile connected to the earth you'll allow the beneficial composting critters that live in the soil to migrate up and down as the seasons change.

Finally, consider the aesthetics of your compost pile and how it fits in with the landscape. While you may think your sprawling, uncontained heap is a magnificent statement of environmental consciousness, your neighbors may not. And although most piles are very well mannered, you may occasionally experience a few off-color odors or small clouds of fruit flies. Not nice if the folks next door have their gas grill just on the other side of the fence.

Don't risk offending—place your pile in a neutral corner if you're going to compost where you're rubbing shoulders with your neighbors. And then bring them a nice wheelbarrow full of finished compost when you see them next spring. Tell them about this wondrous home-made product and see if they don't start their own bin soon.

WHEN TO START

There is no better time to start your compost than now! Composting is a very forgiving process, so there's no reason to hesitate starting a batch right away. Of course, some seasons lend themselves to initiating a new pile. In spring and early summer there's always an abundance of grass clippings, pulled weeds, and hedge prunings. And in the fall there are all those dead leaves to gather. You don't need the ideal balance of greens and browns to start your pile, but it does help when they're both around.

Depending on how cold it gets, the composting process slows down in winter because the composting critters either go dormant or retreat into the soil for protection. In very cold weather, everything grinds to a halt, so there's no need to turn or poke your pile; it may become frozen solid and nearly impossible to move anyway. But even though the microbes are hibernating, the alternating freezes and thaws of winter help raw materials break down mechanically. And once it starts to warm up, all of the microbes and their cousins will return to work with more surface areas to munch on.

During the winter months you may not have much yard waste, but you're still inside cooking and eating and producing lots of kitchen scraps. Just toss them on the pile and hurry back inside. If you keep a basket or bag of leaves on hand and use them to cover up the scraps periodically, you'll have a compost lasagna ready to defrost and rot come spring.

COLD-CLIMATE COMPOSTING

If you want your compost pile to stay active during the winter, buy or build a bin with insulated sides. A black bin situated in a sunny spot can help trap solar radiation during cold spells too. And keep your pile as large as possible so that the heat generated from decomposition will endure. You can also stack bales of straw along the sides of your bin to help retain the heat.

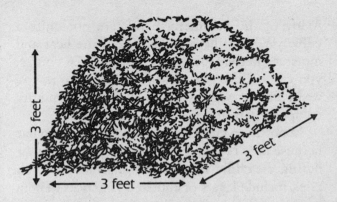

SIZE

A compost pile of any size and dimension will eventually rot. That's a fact of nature. But building a pile that's too big or too small can slow down the composting process. Small piles get plenty of air but don't retain the heat of the decomposition and may dry out frequently. Very tall piles have a tendency to become compacted in the middle, resulting in poor air circulation. They also can be difficult to turn.

The rule of thumb most composters use is to build a pile that's no smaller than one cubic yard—3 feet high by 3 feet wide by 3 feet deep—and no taller than 6 feet. Piles in this range retain heat while allowing adequate air flow.

Many of the commercial bins are not quite a cubic yard, but because they hold the heat and moisture better, they work just fine. Of course, you can build a pile as wide and as long as you wish; this is what is done at most community composting facilities.

In northern climes, big piles are more popular because they're better insulated and stay warmer during the chilly winters. If you go for sky-high piles, include layers of cornstalks or sticks to help keep the pile airier. You can also aerate a tall pile with a ventilator tube.

FILLING THE BIN

So what goes into the big bad compost pile? You start with what's on hand. That probably means grass clippings in spring and summer, autumn leaves in the fall, and kitchen scraps year-round. Details on these three common ingredients follow in another chapter. But don't stop there. There are tons of super-compostable ingredients in and around your house that you can feed into your ever-hungry pile. And by using a wide variety of ingredients, your finished compost will be a richer, more nutritious plant food.

Balance is the key to good compost. Try to include roughly equal amounts of browns (dried carbon-rich ingredients) and greens (juicy nitrogen-rich ingredients) in your pile. By keeping these two in balance, you'll be providing the proper diet for the microbial life-forms that keep your pile composting. Remember also that the finer ground, shredded or even bruised your ingredients are, the quicker they will decompose.

Even though the tiny, hungry bacteria that do the dirty work of decay are everywhere, you'll want to make sure your pile has enough of the right kind to get started. By occasionally adding small amounts of rich garden topsoil, aged manure, or some previously made compost (you can think of these materials as "blacks" to continue the color imagery), you can inoculate your pile with the right stuff and get it cooking quicker. You can also add special compost starters, or *inoculants*, if your pile is sluggish. (See the box, "Compost Condiments," at the end of this chapter.)

There are two basic approaches to combining raw ingredients. To use the lasagna, or layer cake, method, you would alternate layers of browns with layers of greens and include an occasional thin layer of blacks. Other folks go with the tossed salad approach by throwing all of the ingredients together and stirring them until they're well mixed. Either way is fine. Whichever way you choose, it's also a good idea to throw in some bulky things like hedge trimmings, evergreen boughs, or prunings at the bottom of the pile to aid in air circulation.

While you're mixing or layering your ingredients, keep an eye on how wet or dry the pile feels. You want everything to be moist but not sopping wet. If the ingredients are too dry, periodically sprinkle them as you build the heap. If you wait till the heap is completely built to hose it down, the water might not penetrate to all parts of the pile.

You can also add new materials on an ongoing basis to an already established pile. Most single-bin gardeners build an initial pile and then add more ingredients on top as they become available. Even without being turned, the older ingredients at the bottom of the pile become finished compost sooner than the most recent additions. To remove the bottom compost, you might have to disassemble the bin although some bin manufacturers offer units with trap doors at the bottom to make this easier.

Always remember that you can't fail when you make compost. If you don't follow all the suggestions outlined here, you may get a pile that takes a long time to rot or gives off a few smells, but you can always correct these problems later if you want to. Compost is going to happen one way or the other.

MOISTURE

Your compost pile is home to millions of living creatures, all of which need water to decompose effectively. If a pile becomes too dry, the decay process will slow down and the pile won't do much but sit there and desiccate. If there's too much water in your heap, you'll drown out all the wee composting beasties, and you'll also begin to lose nutrients through leaching. The rule of thumb is to keep your pile as moist as a wrung-out sponge. So grab a handful and give it a squeeze every now and then. You'll soon know just by sight when your pile is thirsty.

If your pile becomes waterlogged due to excessive rain, give it a turn with a pitchfork, add some dry material like straw, or cover it up with a plastic tarp or an old rug to ward off additional downpours. You can also spread it out a little if your're composting in an open pile. In wet climates, you might consider building a little roof or cover to protect the pile from the rain, or you can simply invest in a bin with a lid.

If your pile gets dry and dusty, give it a sprinkle with the hose. In consistently arid climates, try to make a little dimple in the top of the heap to gather the little rain that falls.

AIR CIRCULATION

A healthy compost pile needs to breathe. Those diminutive denizens of decomposition require oxygen to weave those raw materials into finished compost. If your pile doesn't get enough air, the aerobic microbes will go home and the slow and stinky anaerobic ones will kick in.

There are several ways to keep your pile breathing freely. First, try not to use too many ingredients that compact easily. Thick layers of finely ground sawdust, unshredded wet leaves, and fresh grass clippings can become compressed into mats that resist decomposition. Keep these ingredients well mixed to prevent them from forming dense impenetrable layers.

Second, build some loft into your pile by adding occasional layers of hedge trimmings, tree prunings, or straw. These bulky materials will keep small air pockets open in the pile. People who build large piles often place old sunflower stalks, tree branches, or ventilating tubes vertically in different parts of their pile to maximize the air circulation (see the box, "Ventilation Tubes," below).

If you want to increase the air circulation even more, you're going to have to get physical with your pile. Turning a pile by hand can be sweaty work, but it's a great way to re-oxygenate the heap and get the outer ingredients into the middle for more even decomposition.

If you have an unenclosed pile, turning is a simple matter. Using a garden fork, you just dig in and rebuild the heap right next to the old one. If you have a multi-bin unit, the process is basically the same. Lift the compost out and into an

empty bin. Some compost bins can be lifted or disassembled easily, allowing you room to turn and remix the materials.

Turning is sometimes not an option. If your bin does not lift off or come apart easily, your best bet is to use the fork to stir the ingredients a little. You can also poke holes in the pile with a pole or broomstick to let more air in. Special compost-turning tools that work well in small bins are also available (see the "Accessories" chapter). If you don't (or can't) turn, stir, poke or prod you'll still get compost but it will take longer to finish and you might experience a few off odors.

VENTILATION TUBES

Find or buy a 4- or 5-foot piece of plastic pipe at least 3 inches wide and drill as many holes in it as you can. Set the pipe vertically into the middle of the beginning pile and add your raw materials around it as you build. The tube will increase the amount of fresh air available to the center of the heap. If your pile is rather wide, use several tubes spaced equally apart.

COMPOST CONDIMENTS

"Psst. Hey, buddy, want to buy some magic composting powder? Guaranteed to ignite your pile in no time."

It's true, special compost activators and inoculants are available that promise to cook your compost quicker. Some provide concentrated amounts of the proper microorganisms. Others add a lot of nitrogen as a microbial food source or change the pH of the pile to encourage desirable bacteria. They are sprinkled and mixed into the pile to speed up your rot pot.

You probably don't need them, though. The proper microorganisms are crawling over everything anyway, so you can just wait until they get up and running. An easy way to ensure a healthy population is to add a few shovelfuls of finished compost from your first pile to your subsequent ones. It's kind of like saving sourdough starter from batch to batch. Finished compost is rich with all those creatures that have already become acclimated to your backyard. Compost tea is another great way to inoculate a new pile (see the box on page 122).

Other compost starters include aged manure, alfalfa meal, cottonseed meal, and blood meal. All are rich in nitrogen, and a sprinkling will jump-start the microbes already in your pile. These activators are cheaper than the commercially made ones and work just as well.

COMPOST UNITS

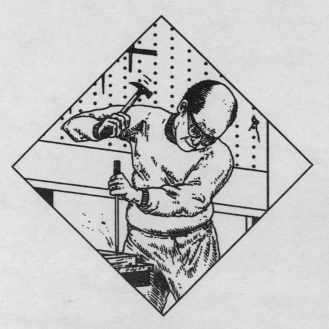

YOU CAN BUILD

The Portable Composter

HERE'S A BIN THAT'S EASY TO MAKE AND can be easily moved about your yard. First get about 11 feet of 3- to 4-foot-wide snow fence, hardware cloth, or other flexible fencing material. Connect the two ends using bits of thick wire as heavy-duty twist ties. If you use hardware cloth, bend the top few inches over to make the unit more rigid and to keep those sharp edges away from your eyes, hands, and sweaters. If you want to turn the pile, simply remove the wire ties and unwrap the fencing. Reconstruct the bin a few feet away and, using a garden fork, move and mix the compost back into the newly formed unit. You can make this simple structure more secure by driving one or more wooden stakes or pieces of old pipe into the ground with a heavy hammer and then attaching the fencing to the poles.

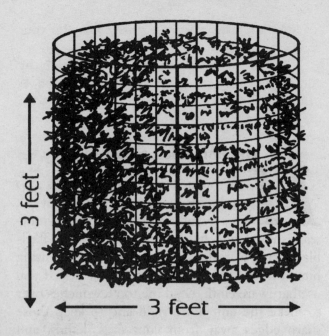

3 feet

3 feet

Recycled Pallet Composter

If you keep your eyes open, you can usually find a source of free discarded wooden shipping pallets in your area. These pallets are typically shallow 4-by 4-foot boxes designed to allow forklifts to move large quantities of goods. Look for them at trucking or shipping companies or home improvement centers. Use rope or wire to attach four pallets together to form a simple sturdy box for your compost.

You can elaborate on this basic design by adding an additional pallet as a bottom or lid. A pallet on the bottom will help increase air flow to the pile and a lid will help retain moisture and keep out nosy dogs. To make it easier to empty the box or turn the heap, drive a few poles through three of the side pallets and into the ground. When you want to turn or empty the bin,

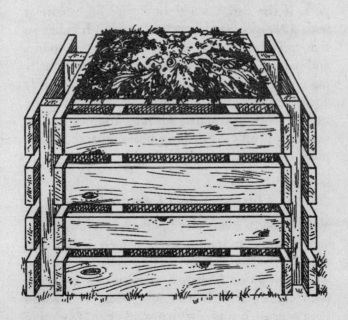

just remove the fourth side and the unit will still stand on its own.

Composter in a Drum

Take a 30- or 40-gallon galvanized metal trash can and drill plenty of ½- to 1-inch holes in the bottom and sides for ventilation. Now set the drum on top of a few staggered concrete blocks so that it is secure and most of the bottom holes are not covered. Add materials and start to compost. If the can has a tight fitting lid, secure it with a bungee cord attached to both handles so that you'll be able to roll the can on its side to mix and aerate. If you don't have a lid, occasionally poke some holes in the compost with a sturdy stick or insert a long ventilation tube down the middle when you start your pile. You can make a ventilation tube by drilling holes up and down a piece of wide plastic pipe.

Chicken Coop Composter

You can make a very airy bin by first creating four square wooden frames from sixteen 3-foot sections of 1- by 2-inch lumber. Use galvanized wood screws or L-shaped metal plates to secure each corner and then attach sheets of chicken wire over each frame with a staple gun. Assemble the four sides into a bin and use hooks and eyes at the top an bottom of each frame to keep it standing. You can make a fifth frame if you need a lid.

Concrete Composter

You can use standard concrete building blocks to build a compost bin of any shape or configuration you want. Stagger the blocks to allow maximum

air circulation and don't use mortar—you'll want to be able to expand or move the structure at some point. You can also stack the blocks on their sides with their holes facing outward to allow even greater air flow.

COMPOST UNITS

YOU CAN BUY

*A*N ASTONISHING NUMBER AND VARIETY of ready-made compost units are on sale these days. It appears that every backyard inventor who had some time on his hands thought up a new and better way to contain compost. Some are very basic bins made of recycled materials while others have special features that can help you make compost faster or more easily. Some are sleek and discreet and will blend in with your landscape while others will surely call attention to themselves. Before you buy any unit, call your local municipality to see if it offers composters to homeowners at reduced rates.

You may find some of the following units at your garden shop or home center. Just about all the rest can be ordered by mail. Prices range from thirty dollars to many hundreds of dollars. Although this list is extensive, it is by no means complete. Composter manufacturers come and go, and models change over the years.

BIO-ORB

This is a ball-shaped bin with a tight-fitting lid that you can roll on the ground to mix and aerate your compost. It comes in two sizes—36 or 44 inches in diameter—and is constructed of 100 percent post-consumer recycled plastic.

Shape Plastics Corp.
1212 Barberry Drive
Janesville, WI 53545
800-888-1232

BIOSTACK

The Biostack is three open-ended recycled polyethylene tiers that you can stack as you fill the bin and then unstack when you want to turn or use the compost. This composter holds 13 cubic feet and comes with a hinged lid. Extra tiers are available if you want a taller pile.

Smith & Hawken
Two Arbor Lane
Box 6900
Florence, KY 41022-6900
800-981-9888

BRAVE NEW COMPOSTER

You can determine the size of this composter—from 12 to 24 cubic feet—as you set it up. Two plastic cones are included—one on the bottom to allow greater air circulation and the other on the top to retain generated heat. Made from green or black 100 percent post-consumer recycled plastic that is UV stabilized.

Nature's Backyard
241 Duchaine Blvd.
New Bedford, MA 02745
800-853-2525

CANDO COMPOSTER

This tumbler is a polyethylene barrel suspended over a PVC pipe frame. The barrel is a recycled food container that is spun head over heels. It comes in two sizes—6 and 7 bushels.

CanDo Composter Company
5990 Old Stilesboro Road
Acworth, GA 30101
404-974-0046

CEDAR COMPOST BIN

The cedar planks that form the sides of this unit are held in place by four 16 gauge steel posts that are driven into the ground. You can purchase the posts by themselves and use your own lumber to build a bin to whatever dimensions you need. Boards slip in and out for easy access.

The Natural Gardening Company
217 San Anselmo Avenue
San Anselmo, CA 94960
707-766-9303

COL-MET COMPOST BIN
Constructed of 22-gauge galvinized steel, this large (20 cubic feet) bin measures 36 by 36 by 30 inches. All six sides are ventilated and can be lifted up for easy turning.

Collier Metal Specialties, Inc.
715 Easy Street
Garland, TX 75042
(214) 494-3900

COMPOSTUMBLER
An old favorite of gardeners, this tumbling unit is an 18-bushel galvanized steel drum that sits on top of a sturdy steel frame. A uniquely designed geared crank makes turning a breeze, and the side door has latches for easy opening and closing.

PBM Group
160 Koser Road
Lititz, PA 17543
717-627-4300

THE COVERED BRIDGE COMPOSTING BIN

This simple but well-designed bin is made from a sheet of thick black HPDE plastic that is 100 percent post-consumer and UV stabilized. This bin can be either 3 or 4 feet in diameter and will hold 18 to 30 cubic feet of materials. It features intake slits at the bottom and cutouts for handles at the top.

Covered Bridge Organic
Box 91
Jefferson, OH 44047
(216) 576-5515

E-Z SPIN COMPOSTER

This classically designed metal tumbler is supported by a sturdy steel frame. Two sliding doors open to accommodate 11 cubic feet of raw materials. Convenient handles are used to spin the unit.

Troy-Bilt Manufacturing Company
102nd Street & 9th Avenue
Troy, NY 12180
800-828-5500

FLOWTRON CB40 AND CB50

Two well-made units constructed of recycled black polyethylene that is UV stabilized. The CB40 holds 14 cubic feet and has two hinged bottom doors for access. The CB50 has removable bottom slats instead. Two or more CB50s can be interlocked together to create a multi-bin unit. Flowtron also sells an aerating tool.

Flowtron Outdoor Products
2 Main Street
Melrose, MA 02176
617-324-8400

GARDENER'S GOLD COMPOST TUMBLER

This tumbler is a 55-gallon black polyethylene barrel suspended on a frame of UV-stabilized polyvinyl chloride pipe. It features a lock-lever lid and is tumbled head over heels. Holds 9 bushels.

Age Old Organics
Box 1556
Boulder, CO 80306
303-499-0201

GREEN CONE FOOD WASTE RECYCLER

This is a double-walled, heat-trapping polyethylene cone that is partially buried in the ground. It is uniquely designed to accept only

food waste and because it is so tightly constructed, it can compost meat, fish and dairy
wastes without odors or pests. Requires no
turning and needs to be emptied only once
every year or two.

Solarcone, Inc.
Box 67
Seward, IL 61077-0067
800-807-6527

GREEN GENIE COMPOSTER

Features of this 53-gallon bin include an
adjustable lid to regulate the air flow and a perfo-
rated bottom that allows air and worms to enter
in but keeps rodents out. This composter is constructed of reprocessed polyethylene.

Bonar Plastics
35 Andrew Street
Newman, GA 30283
404-251-8264

GREEN JOHANNA COMPOSTER RECYCLER

This Swedish-designed plastic bin is rodent-
proof, but it allows worms to enter and leave.
Because it uses a passive ventilation system, this
unit is able to process meat and dairy waste also.
It holds 11 cubic feet of material.

Earthmade Products
Box 609
Jasper, IN 47547-06609
800-843-1819

Green Magic Tumbler

This barrel-shaped tumbler is supported by an aluminum frame and is designed to be spun head over heels. The container is made from 75 percent post-consumer recycled plastic and features a screw-on lid and a handle at the bottom for easier spinning.

Gardener's Supply
128 Intervale Road
Burlington, VT 05401-2850
802-863-4535

Novawood Compost Bin

This traditionally designed bin holds up to 27 cubic feet of materials. The slatted sides allow excellent air circulation, and it's made entirely from 100 percent mixed recycled plastics by a company that specializes in environmentally sound products.

Obex, Inc.
Box 1253
Stamford, CT 06904
800-876-8735

NO-TURN COMPOSTER

This cylindrical bin comes with four ventilation tubes that you insert as you fill it up. It also comes with a large plastic disc that sits on top of your materials and helps retain the heat generated by decay. It's made of recycled plastics that are UV stabilized and can hold up to 14.8 cubic feet.

Gardener Equipment Company
Box 106
Juneau, WI 53039
800-393-0333

NUTRI CUBE

Made from rot-resistant cedarwood, this traditional slatted bin comes in three sizes: 22, 56, and 90 cubic feet. It can be assembled quickly and can be emptied through a hinged bottom panel.

Siewart Cabinet
2740 31st Avenue South
Minneapolis, MN 55406
612-721-4456

ROLLING COMPOST MACHINE

This octagonal ball features internal blades to help break up and mix the compost. Made of UV-inhibited plastic, this unit also features a locking lid, extra-thick walls, and convenient handles. It holds 11 cubic feet of material and is made to be pushed around the yard

Gardener's Supply
128 Intervale Road
Burlington, VT 05401-2850
800-863-1700

RUBBERMAID COMPOSTER

You assemble this roomy (18 cubic feet) and sturdy rectangular composter from six pieces of interlocking plastic. It features a removable lid, a bottom door for compost removal, and plenty of side louvers for air circulation. The walls are double-insulated for better cold-weather performance.

Rubbermaid Specialty Products, Inc.
1147 Akron Road
Wooster, OH 44691
800-347-3114

SPEEDIBIN

This rodent-resistant bin features a large front

door and a lid for easy loading and unloading. A baked enamel finish covers the metal walls, and a steel mesh floor keeps out rodents. It holds 14 cubic feet of compostable materials.

Speedibins
3930 Hobbs Street
Victoria, BC V8N4C9
604-477-0148

SWISHER COMPOSTERS
Made from recycled galvanized steel, these box-shaped tumblers are turned by solar-powered motors. Air vents are adjustable, and a simple automatic watering system distributes moisture while the tumbler rotates. Several sizes are available, including one that is manually turned.

Swisher Mower and Machine Company
Box 67
Warrensburg, MO 64093
800-222-8183

TUMBLEBUG
Shaped like a geodesic ball, this composter comes in a diameter of 37, 43, or 50 inches and is meant to be rolled about on the ground. It is constructed of UV-stabilized, 100 percent recycled

HDPE with galvanized steel straps for support. Long bolts on the inside help break up clumps of compost during tumbling.

Tumblebug
2029 North 23rd
Boise, ID 83702
800-531-0102

YARDCYCLER
This heavy plastic bin has a lid designed to let in rainfall but keep out rodents. Each side has two wide slots to allow you to lift and mix the materials inside with a garden fork. This bin can hold up to 15 cubic feet.

The Toro Company
8111 Lindale Avenue South
Minneapolis, MN 55420
800-348-2424

MATERIALS FOR COMPOSTING

*T*HERE'S JUST SO DARN MUCH STUFF YOU can throw into your compost pile. Start off by including all your yard waste—prunings, clippings, weeds, and leaves. Then bring out your kitchen scraps—peelings, tea bags,

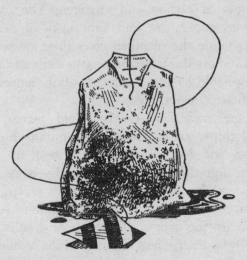

coffee grounds, and moldy bread. And if you start looking around the neighborhood, you're sure to find even more organic matter to snatch from the trash stream and redirect to your magic pile. You can always find more stuff to compost, and this chapter will give you some ideas about where to look. We'll also tell you about the few things you should never compost.

BROWNS AND GREENS

All of the ingredients that you might consider throwing onto your heap contain varying amounts of carbon and nitrogen. The carbon provides energy to your tiny army of decomposers while the nitrogen gives them protein to grow and divide. When these two elements are in a reasonable balance, decomposition happens in an efficient, orderly way.

Some materials—sawdust, old leaves, and wood chips, for example—are naturally high in carbon and low in nitrogen. These are your brown ingredients. Other materials—grass clippings, fresh leaves, and kitchen scraps, for instance—are low in carbon but high in nitrogen. These are the greens. If browns or greens were just left by themselves, decomposition would still occur, but it might take a long time. Put them together, however, and you've got Fred and Ginger—two well-matched partners ready to tango. Always try to have both colors represented in your pile. You don't have to do any fancy calculations; just judge the amounts roughly equal by weight and use your senses to determine when your pile is out of balance.

Beyond the Backyard

Once you've collected your home and yard refuse, keep an open mind and an open eye for unusual or overlooked organic matter that may be readily available in your neck of the woods. You'll find a lot of manufacturing by-products in the following list. See if you can locate some of your region's specialties and add them to your home compost cooker. After all, variety is not only the spice of life, it's also a great way to make superior compost. By including an assortment of materials in your heap you invite more kinds of microorganisms to join the feast, and you'll end up with a compost that's richer in micronutrients and better for your plants.

Of course, you should always ask at the source about possible contamination of any materials you plan to truck home. A stable manager may have sprayed an insecticide on the horse bedding you want to haul away. Or your neighbor may have dosed his lawn heavily with an herbicide

A WORD ABOUT RATIOS

Some materials are high in carbon and low in nitrogen; others are just the reverse. A few materials are evenly balanced. Professional composters like to know the specific ratio of these two elements in any raw material so they can provide a balanced diet for their microorganisms.

This ratio is usually written C:N, where the first number is the amount of carbon present to every one part of nitrogen. An ideal ratio for microbial munchers is between 20:1 and 30:1. If there's too much carbon in the mixture, as in a pile made up only of dead tree leaves (40:1), compost will happen but not quickly and without much heat generated. Too much nitrogen in a pile, like one made exclusively of grass clippings (10:1), means quick decomposition, but the excess nitrogen will become gaseous and won't fortify the finished compost. If you mix equal parts clippings and leaves, however, the result will be a perfect blend of materials with a final ratio of 25:1

You don't need to know the specific ratio of your materials, but it does help to keep in mind which ingredients have higher or lower ratios. That way you can balance different materials for peak efficiency.

before he mowed and offered you the clippings. Even though some research shows that most pesticides break down in a hot pile, it's always best to play it safe. So if in doubt, leave it out.

MATERIALS FOR COMPOSTING

ALFALFA.   This protein-rich legume is grown throughout North America primarily as a livestock food. Its deep roots penetrate the soil, bringing up valuable buried nutrients. Alfalfa is generally available at feed stores as hay, meal, and pellets. The hay is too expensive for composting, but spoiled hay—bales damaged by rain and useless as feed— can often be had for almost nothing. In all its forms, alfalfa is high in nitrogen and can help compensate for other less potent materials.

APPLE POMACE.   Apple pomace is the wet, fragrant residue of skins, seeds, and pulp left over from pressing apples for juice or cider. Although it is somewhat low in nitrogen, the large quantity of seeds will benefit your compost by providing significant nutrients. Pomace is moist and dense and can easily become compacted and smelly if not mixed with drier, more absorbent materials such as fall leaves or hay. It is also notorious for attracting bees and yellow jackets, so mix it in as soon as possible. Because apples are often sprayed with heavy-duty pesticides, it's best to ask a few questions before loading up your buckets.

ASHES.   Wood ashes from a fireplace or stove can be added to your pile or sprinkled directly on your garden. They are especially high in potassium, though, so use them only in moderation—too much and your plants may become stunted. Sift the ashes to remove large chunks before using and don't let the ashes sit out in the rain or the nutrients will leach out. Wood ashes can also be dusted on plants as an organic pest deterrent.

Don't use coal ashes. They usually contain large amounts of sulfur and iron that can injure your flowers and vegetables. Used charcoal briquettes don't decay much at all—ancient charcoal from primitive cooking fires is still being found—and will keep popping up unchanged, so don't bother tossing them in your heap.

BAGASSE.   This is the waste product left over from cane sugar extraction. Look for bagasse at sugar refineries in the Deep South. It is very high in carbon, almost like sawdust, and therefore needs to be mixed with a good nitrogen source for best results. Its fluffy quality can help keep a pile light and airy.

BANANA PEELS.   If you live near a banana processing plant or a bakery that uses lots of bananas, you can take advantage of all those slippery skins and stems. Because this fragrant residue rots quickly, it can attract fruit flies, so make sure you cover it up immediately with dried leaves or sawdust. Banana residue is moderately rich in nutrients, especially potash.

BASIC SLAG.   When iron ore is smelted, impurities rise to the surface of the molten metal and form slag. When this crusty substance is skimmed off, cooled, and ground into a fine blackish dust, it is used by farmers as a soil mineral supplement. In the compost pile it breaks down slowly and increases the nutritive quality of the finished compost. Slag is usually quite high in calcium and other minerals, but it varies considerably from batch to batch. Avoid batches containing too much sulfur as this can overacidify your pile.

BEET WASTE.   After the sugar is extracted from sugar beets, the potassium-rich residue is dried and sold as a livestock food. If you live near a sugar beet extractor, ask if you can haul some away. You might also find dried beet pulp in a feed store.

BLOOD MEAL. Dried blood meal is a slaughterhouse by-product. Because it is water-soluble and nitrogen-rich, it is a very potent fertilizer and compost activator. It is expensive, but a little sprinkling of blood meal through the pile will stimulate microbial activity.

BONE MEAL. Bone meal is just what it sounds like—the powdered bones of slaughtered animals. Bone meal is naturally high in nitrogen and phosphorus. Raw bone meal has more nitrogen than steamed bone meal but less phosphorus. Bone black is burned bone meal that's used as a filter during sugar refining. Often used as a soil amendment for flower bulbs, bone meal can also be added in limited quantities to compact your pile.

CASTOR POMACE. Castor beans are grown in the Deep South for use in making castor oil. When the beans are squeezed, castor pomace is what is left over. High in nitrogen and phosphorus, castor pomace is almost as helpful as manure is in getting a pile to cook.

CITRUS WASTES. If you live near an orange, lemon, or grapefruit processor, check the availability of free citrus pulp. You may also find it in a dried form at feed stores. Although rich in potassium, it may contain significant levels of pesticides. You can use citrus rinds from your kitchen, but they will take a long time to break down. Remember to cut them up before adding them to your pile.

COFFEE. Coffee grounds are a very welcome addition to your pile. Earthworms love them terribly, and they also help deodorize your heap a bit. However, if you add a lot of grounds without mixing them in, they can ferment and attract fruit flies. Keep a small bucket by your office coffee machine and bring it home every few days. Don't bother separating out the paper filters—they'll disintegrate shortly. You can use coffee grounds as a mulch around acid-loving plants such as blueberries and azaleas, too. Also, ask your coffee roaster to save you any burned beans or coffee chaff.

CORNCOBS. Corncobs are the slowpokes of the compost pile. They seem to take forever to rot, so chop or shred them before you toss them in. If you don't, they'll still contribute to the pile's health by allowing more air circulation. Cornstalks are also very slow to rot unless they're first ground up in a chipper-shredder.

COTTON WASTE. Also known as gin trash, this is what's left of the cotton plant after the bolls have been harvested. Because arsenic compounds are often sprayed on cotton fields, make sure you ask about toxins before hauling the waste away. Cotton stalks are also available, but they're slow to rot unless first chipped or shredded.

COTTONSEED MEAL. When cottonseed oil is extracted from the seeds, you're left with cottonseed meal. Also known as oil cake or seedcake, it's very rich in protein and other nutrients and is commonly sold as an expensive animal feed. Because cotton is a nonfood crop, it can contain high levels of pesticides.

FEATHERS. Turkey, chicken, and duck feathers are rich with nitrogen and may be available at a poultry processor. Because they shed water so effectively, hose them down thoroughly when mixing them into your pile.

FELT WASTE. If you live near a hat factory, inquire about felt and wool waste. This high-nitrogen by-product can get a slow pile in high gear, but because it is quite dry, it needs to be thoroughly moistened in the pile.

FISH WASTE AND FISH MEAL.   Easily available at canneries and processors, fish waste can be a valuable source of nitrogen and trace minerals. It does, however, have a very strong smell and needs to be incorporated quickly into a pile with lots of high-carbon materials such as wood shavings or sawdust. If left standing alone, it will quickly putrefy and attract rodents and flies. Fish skins and bones from last night's supper can also be handled in this manner. You can also bury fish waste directly in your garden, but plant it deep to keep vermin away. Fish meal (dried and ground up fish parts) is another nutritious by-product, although it's more expensive than fish waste. It's not as smelly, but it may still attract neighborhood dogs and cats to your yard.

GARDEN REFUSE.   All of your spent plants, thinned seedlings, and deadheaded flowers should make the quick trip to your bin. Pulled weeds, with some exceptions, are also fine, but first read the two "weeds" entries at the end of this chapter. Don't include plants that you suspect are diseased or gone to seed unless you plan on having a super-hot pile.

GRAPE WASTES.   Visit a vineyard or a winery during pressing time and you may walk away with bags of grape residue. It will most likely be wet and messy, but it will decompose rather quickly into your pile.

GRASS CLIPPINGS. What do most people do with their grass clippings after mowing? They stuff them into plastic bags and have them hauled at great expense to a crowded landfill where it takes years for them to breakdown. What a waste! They're throwing away tons and tons of one of composting's most valuable ingredients. Grass clippings are already shredded, they're easy to handle, and they are available just about everywhere. They break down quickly, contain as much nitrogen as manure, and can also be used as mulching material. They deserve much more respect than most people care to give them.

Fresh grass clippings, however, do tend to clump together if just heaped up alone. Make sure you mix them up with a brown material (like dead leaves, straw, or wood chips) and you'll be rewarded with some mighty fine compost. If you have lots and lots of clippings, it's better to let them dry out on the lawn before you rake them up. They'll lose a little nitrogen, but they won't clump so much.

Don't forget to look next door for more of this valuable resource. Your non-composting neigh-

MULCHING MOWER TO THE RESCUE

Most older lawn mowers either collect grass clippings in a bag or spew them about the yard to be raked up later. But more and more of the newer models are mulching mowers—machines designed to finely shred the grass clippings and blow them back into the lawn, where they decompose quickly. Within a week, those former clippings are fertilizing your lawn and you're spared the chore of raking or emptying the mower bag. Additionally, those tiny clippings will help rejuvenate your soil's beneficial life-forms and act as a water-saving mulch to boot. For best results with a mulching mower, cut your grass frequently and only when it's dry. Set the height of your mower to remove only about one-third of the grass blades' total length.

bors will gladly send their clippings in your direction. Landscapers are also usually delighted to drop off some or all of their excess clippings. As you would do with any imported ingredient, first ask your donors if their lawns were sprayed with herbicides or pesticides before they were mowed. Although it is generally believed that most lawn chemicals break down in the composting process, don't take chances. A heavy residue of broadleaf weed killers can hurt your lettuce and lobelias too. Get your clippings from the dandelion-loving folks on the block.

And if you've decided to get rid of your lawn altogether, don't hesitate to top off your pile with the excess sod. Just make sure to put it in upside down so it will rot rather than grow. This is also a nifty way to keep excess water off the compost heap in rainy weather.

GREENSAND. Normally sold as a soil amendment, greensand is also a fine addition to your compost pile. Mined from ancient undersea beds, it contains high levels of potassium and other micronutrients.

HAIR. Yes, it's a little creepy, but hair can contain up to ten times as much nitrogen as manure! You can collect it from beauty salons, barbershops, or pet groomers—although you may get some strange looks when you make your request. For safety's sake, avoid salons where a lot of chemicals are used. Because hair tends to repel water, it needs to be moistened well or mixed with wetter ingredients to break down.

HAY AND STRAW.   Because of their high carbon content, dried hay or straw can be a little demanding on a pile. But they're an ideal foil for high-nitrogen manure. Mix them together whenever possible. Rain-spoiled hay—so-called gray hay left in the field and unfit for livestock—and weathered gray straw are available in some rural regions. Straw's little tubes will also help keep your pile breathing better.

HOOF AND HORN MEAL.   Another slaughterhouse by-product, hoof and horn meal is similar to hair (it's actually compressed hair, if you like) and very high in nitrogen. Sprinkle the finely ground type on your pile and stir. The coarser, chunkier kind can be used also, but it will decompose more slowly and may attract flies.

HOPS.   Spent hops from breweries are a fine source of nitrogen for your compost. They are usually available wet, so mix them with some dry ingredients to avoid anaerobic decomposition. Hops add a wonderful fragrance to your pile—if you like beery smells. You can also spread them directly on your garden beds and work them in or use them as a long-lasting mulch. Look for spent malt also.

HULLS. Depending on where you live, you may find that the outer hulls of buckwheat, oats, and rice are available to you at no cost. They tend to be rich in potassium, decompose fairly readily, and are easy to handle. Their light, fluffy texture helps to puff up your pile also. Avoid sunflower hulls, though—they contain a natural herbicide that withstands composting and can later prevent your vegetable and flower seeds from germinating.

KITCHEN REFUSE. When you compost your kitchen scraps, you benefit in two ways. First, if you've always thrown away your melon rinds and onion skins, your trash cans will now be lighter and less smelly. Second, you'll be providing your composting critters with a wider variety of new food sources. And they in turn will create a richer, more nutritious plant food.

So start redirecting those carrot shavings, tea bags, coffee grounds, apple cores, and banana peels to your friendly heap. Don't forget to include stale baked goods, corncobs, and that inedible fruitcake your niece stuck you with last year. If you make fresh juices, your pile will love the leftover pulp

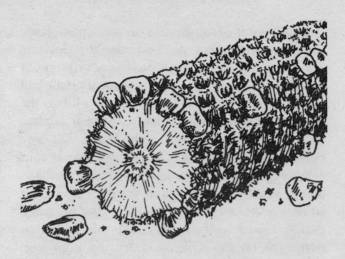

and it will disappear in a flash. Remember to cut or break up chunky or tough things like grapefruit rinds, cabbage cores, and corncobs for easier assimilation into your pile. Don't neglect commercial sources of kitchen scraps—cullings from the local supermarket, hotel, or restaurant may be available just by asking the manager.

Some kitchen scraps such as meat, bones, fat, grease, and oil are not suitable for composting. These items can be just as tough for your pile to digest as they are for you. They take a long time to decompose and can attract unwanted visitors in the meantime. Eggshells are the exception; they break down quickly and add calcium to the compost.

There are many ways to collect and use your

kitchen waste. Many people keep a small plastic container on the counter or under the sink and bring it to the pile every few days. A rinsed-out recycled ice-cream container or a small plastic pail will work well for this purpose. Keep a lid on the container to discourage insects. Special kitchen compost containers with tight-fitting lids and built-in carbon air filters are also available. If your compost pile is in the far reaches of your yard and there's snow on the ground, consider keeping a larger bucket in a cold spot such as your unheated garage. Occasionally sprinkle a little sawdust or peat moss on top to keep it dry and odor-free. When you do add a significant amount of kitchen scraps to a pile, cover them or stir them in to reduce visits by fruit flies and mice.

You can also bury your kitchen scraps directly into your garden beds. Just make sure they are well covered with soil so they don't draw in the neighbors' dogs.

LEATHER DUST.   Often available from tanneries and leather-goods factories, leather dust is a good source of nitrogen and phosphorus, so you may see it for sale in some garden shops. Chromium, a heavy metal, is used in tanning processes, however, so some batches of leather dust may not be good for your home pile. Make inquiries before taking any home.

LEAVES. Autumn leaves are beautiful to most people, but to composters they're gorgeous! Not only do they delight the eye with their wild colors, but they are one of the finest materials to use in compost. They are typically loaded with minerals brought up from the tree's deep roots and are a natural, convenient source of carbon for any pile. Their light flaky texture also helps keep your heap light and airy. Many homeowners persist in dumping or burning this wonderful natural resource. Don't make that mistake—use your valuable fall leaves for compost and mulch.

You can add whole dead leaves directly to your compost pile. Their high carbon-to-nitrogen ratio makes them a good foil for kitchen refuse, grass clippings, and manure. But if you add too many of them at once—and this is how they usually fall from the trees—they will become matted and soggy and will take longer to decompose. If you do have a lot of leaves, it's best to shred them before incorporating them into your compost.

One simple way to shred fall leaves is to run a bagging mower over them where they lie. You'll fill the bag with nicely chopped leaves that are perfect for your pile or for mulching your rosebushes. If you have a leaf blower, you might be able to turn it into a leaf vacuum using the discharge bag to collect the shredded material.

String trimmers (weed-whackers) can also be called upon to chop up dead leaves, especially if you can keep the leaves in some sort of big container like an old pickle barrel or a child's wading pool. Special equipment (see "Accessories" chapter) is also available to process dead leaves. Leaves take up much less space once they're shredded.

Shredded leaves are also an excellent mulch for your garden. By covering the soil around established plants, the mulch will retard the growth of weeds and conserve moisture. Use leaf mulch to cover up any fall root crops and to nestle some hardy greens in for the long winter.

If you're truly overwhelmed by an enormous number of autumn leaves, you can compost them, unshredded, by themselves and let nature run its course. Just heap them together in an open pile or in a simple wire bin, to keep them from blowing about, and then wet them thoroughly. In about two years you should have a crumbly black material known as leaf mold. It's not quite as nutritious for plants as compost, but it is a marvelous soil conditioner. You can also steal from this stash of carbon-rich leaves to balance your compost pile throughout the year. For easy access you can also store the leaves in bags or trash cans right next to your pile.

Still another way of using leaves to build up your soil is to dig or till them directly into your garden beds. Because decomposing leaves can lock up some of the nitrogen in the soil, dig them in before winter so they have time to break down before your spring planting. Alternately, sprinkle a little high-nitrogen material such as manure or blood meal along with the leaves to keep your soil in balance.

Almost all deciduous trees are excellent leaf sources, but a few species—including live oak, southern magnolia, and holly trees—produce leaves that are too tough and leathery for easy composting. Avoid the leaves, nuts, and sawdust from the black walnut tree, too, as they contain a natural plant poison that survives composting. Eucalyptus leaves also contain an oil that can be toxic to other plants. And it goes without saying that no part of a poison ivy, oak, or sumac plant should be included in your compost pile.

MANURE. Animal manure is one of the finest materials you can add to any compost pile for two reasons—it contains large amounts of both nitrogen and beneficial microbes. Manure has been used for centuries as a field fertilizer and a compost igniter. Manure for composting can come from bats, sheep, ducks, pigs, goats, cows, pigeons, and any other vegetarian animal. As a rule of thumb, you should avoid manure from carnivores, as it can contain dangerous pathogens.

Some manure, such as horse, sheep, and poultry waste, is considered "hot" when it's fresh. This means it is so rich in nutrients that it can burn the tender roots of young plants or overheat a compost pile, killing off earthworms and friendly bacteria. If left to age a little, however, these manures are fine to use.

Manure is easier to transport and safer to use if it is rotted, aged, or composted before it's used. Layer manure with carbon-rich brown materials such as straw or leaves to keep your pile in balance. And don't forget to wash your hands after handling manure.

NUTSHELLS.   Shells from peanuts are fine and dandy but walnut, pecan, and almond shells are very slow to rot, so add them sparingly.

PAPER AND CARDBOARD.   You can compost paper, but not in great quantities due to its very high carbon content. And with as much paper as most households discard, it makes better environmental sense to recycle it whenever possible. There has also been concern over the years about the heavy metals used in colored ink, but most researchers now feel that the concentrations are very low and should not cause concern.

The trick to composting paper is to shred it

as fine as possible before putting it in the pile. If left unshredded, it can block the movement of air and water necessary for healthy decomposition. Large quantities of paper suitable for composting are often available at offices where memos and reports are routinely shredded before they're discarded. Don't add too much paper at once unless you have a good source of nitrogen, such as manure, to balance the excess carbon.

All kinds of paper (magazines, newsprint, etc.) can also be used as a practical garden mulch. Lay sheets of paper down around established plants, wet the sheets thoroughly, and cover them with soil or rocks to keep them from blowing away. You can even use layers of paper when you convert a lawn into a garden bed. Place several layers right on top of the sod and cover them with several inches of topsoil or compost. You can plant right through holes in the paper while the grass dies over a period of time.

Cardboard is also compostable, but it must be shredded or torn into small pieces. Worms seem to have an affinity for cardboard and the glues used are generally degradable.

PEAT MOSS.   Peat moss doesn't contain a lot of nutrients, but it's a marvelous soil conditioner. It's light, fluffy texture and prodigious water-retaining ability are legendary. You can compost peat, but it is better suited for directly improving poor soil and propagating plants. If you like, keep a bag by your pile and sprinkle it on top to deter outbreaks of fruit flies.

PINE NEEDLES.   These take a fairly long time to decompose, but they help improve the overall texture of a compost pile. In very large quantities, pine needles can acidify your compost—good if you plan to use the finished product on acid-loving plants.

PRUNINGS AND HEDGE TRIMMINGS.   These woody items take a long time to break down, but an occasional thin layer of short segments can help keep the pile loftier and increase air circulation. Watch out for rose and raspberry prunings—the thorns don't rot as fast as the branches. Shred these and all other trimmings for best results.

ROCK DUST.   Rock dust is just that—the fine powdered by-product of granite and marble quarries. It dissolves quickly into the pile but releases its valuable minerals slowly over a period of years. Rock dust can also be applied directly to garden beds. Use a respirator and apply the dust on a calm, windless day.

SAWDUST. Sawdust is almost all carbon and is very slow to break down. Apply it in layers no more than one inch thick. Very fine sawdust, such as you might get from sanding, can get matted if you add too much at once. You can find sawdust at a lumber mill or gather some from areas where a chain saw has been used. Do not use any sawdust from pressure-treated wood.

SEAWEED AND KELP. Coastal composters can treat their piles to any amounts of kelp and other types of seaweed that washes ashore. Seaweed contains many important trace nutrients and decomposes quickly. If you add a lot of it, use a hose to wash off the salt before sending it to the pile.

SHELLS. Ground-up clam, oyster, or lobster shells may be available near the coast and can be a good source of minerals to your compost. Whole seashells will do nothing but remind you of your last vacation.

TOBACCO STEMS. The discarded stems of tobacco leaves are just fine for compost, but do not use the resulting compost on any crops that are related to tobacco such as tomatoes, peppers, eggplants, and potatoes. They may become infected with tobacco mosaic virus (TMV), an organism that isn't destroyed in the composting process and that can be passed on to plants in the same family.

TOFU FACTORY WASTE. After tofu or soymilk is made, a soybean paste called okara is left over. A softly fragrant addition to your compost, okara is wet and will decompose rapidly.

WEEDS. Weeds can be composted with a few exceptions. If the weeds have formed seed heads, a cool pile will not kill the seeds and they may come back to haunt you. They can be destroyed, however, if you work them into the center of a very hot pile. Also, some weeds like quack grass, Johnson grass, and bittersweet can spread by means of pieces of their roots or rhizomes. Exclude them from your pile also.

WOOD CHIPS. Depending on how coarse they are, wood chips can be slow to rot, but they can help keep the pile a little airier. Use them in moderation. Wood chips are also a great material to spread over your garden paths.

FUN THINGS TO COMPOST

Cotton from vitamin bottles, hair from your golden retriever, dryer lint (especially if your clothes are mostly cotton), stale Twinkies, old houseplants, dead bugs, faded flower arrangements, candy bars, Christmas trees, and wine corks—all can be added to your compost pile. Larger and tougher items will need to be shredded first.

DO NOT ADD THESE MATERIALS

COAL ASHES.   These may contain high amounts of sulfur or iron, which can injure plants.

CHEMICAL FERTILIZERS.   Commercial synthetic plant fertilizers won't speed up your pile and might damage the beneficial microbes already at work.

CONTAMINATED MATERIALS.   Anything that's been sprayed with herbicides, pesticides, fungicides, or other harsh chemicals. Always inquire at the source before bringing outside materials into your yard. If you aren't sure about the cleanliness of the material, be suspicious.

DISEASED OR INSECT-INFESTED PLANTS. Many plant diseases and insect eggs or larvae can survive even the high temperatures of a thermophilic compost pile.

HUMAN WASTE. Even though human waste has been used to fertilize crops in Asia for centuries, it can contain dangerous pathogens. Healthy human urine is generally sterile and contains significant amounts of nitrogen but most folks prefer to get nitrogen into their pile from other sources.

INERT OBJECTS. Don't use things that won't decay, like plastic, glass, aluminum, or synthetic fabrics.

MEAT, BONES, OIL, FAT, GREASE, AND DIARY PRODUCTS. All of these take too long to break down and will often attract pests and vermin.

PET WASTE. Cat and dog feces can, very occasionally, contain dangerous microorganisms that can affect both you and your food plants.

POISONOUS PLANTS. All parts of the poison ivy, poison oak, and poison sumac plant can cause a severe rash in sensitive individuals. Other plants such as black walnut and eucalyptus contain toxins that harm other plants.

SLUDGE. This residue from commercial sewage plants may contain high amounts of heavy metals and disease organisms. Some sludge is marketed commercially to gardeners, but it should not be used on any edible crops.

TOXIC CHEMICALS. Your compost pile is not a chemical dump. Never add cleaners, old medicines, paint, solvents, or any other household chemicals; they could kill the beneficial bacteria in your pile and come back to haunt you in your garden. Call your local sanitation department for information about proper disposal of toxic wastes.

VACUUM CLEANER DUST. This dust is usually fine and composts quite easily, but if your house is older, it may contain chips of lead paint.

WEEDS. Any weeds that have formed seed heads should not be composted. Toss them in their own separate pile or burn them. Weeds with tough creeping roots such as quack grass, Canada

Thistle, Johnson grass, Bermuda grass, ground ivy, oxeye daisy, and mugwort can enjoy the winter in a warm pile and return with a vengeance in the spring. Keep them out!

USING
COMPOST

*Y*OU'VE DONE IT. YOU'VE COLLECTED and stacked and watered and waited. You've watched your pile heat up and shrink down as all those unwanted waste products melded into a beautiful, dark, crumbly soil. So

now that it's finished, you're probably asking yourself, "Just what is all this homemade compost good for?" The answer is everything grown under the sun.

First, compost is the ultimate garden fertilizer. You may know this firsthand if you've witnessed a hale and hearty volunteer tomato, squash, or potato plant shooting out of the pile. Well-made compost contains virtually all the nutrients a living plant needs and delivers them in a slow-release manner over a period of years. Compost made with a wide variety of ingredients will provide an even more nutritious meal to your growing plants. Using compost instead of synthetic chemical fertilizers is like giving your kids a well-balanced home-cooked meal instead of some overpackaged, expensive junk food.

Second, compost is the best material available to enliven your soil no matter where you live. Building soil vitality is a basic tenet of organic gardening. Organic farmers around the world will testify that healthier soil grows healthier plants that naturally resist disease, insects, and other environmental pressures. By spreading compost on your garden beds and berry bushes, you are creating a soil teeming with beneficial microbes. These miniature machines will continue to digest raw materials and fight plant diseases for years to come.

Third, finished compost improves the texture and quality of any soil. The fibrous texture of compost fluffs up dense clay soils and helps sandy, porous soils hold moisture better. Compost helps plants through times of drought because it retains up to ten times its weight in water. It also prevents erosion of our diminishing topsoil by wind and water and helps keep the pH balanced.

HOMEMADE COMPOST VERSUS CHEMICAL FERTILIZERS

No bag of synthetic 10-10-10 fertilizer can compare to the life-giving properties in an equal amount of compost. But thousands of tons of these petroleum-based chemicals are still produced daily and used by conventional farmers as a quick way to boost the productivity of thin, lifeless soil.

The manufacture of chemical fertilizers demands enormous amounts of energy and natural resources, and unfortunately, much of this chemical mixture ends up running off farm fields to pollute our streams and lakes. Perhaps most ironically, synthetic fertilizer has been the prime ingredient in the manufacture of terrorists bombs.

Adding compost to your garden is a long-term investment—it becomes a permanent part of the soil structure, helping to feed future plantings in years to come. Just about every month researchers around the world discover some new advantage to growing crops with compost.

Knowing When Your Compost Is Ready

Compost can take anywhere from two weeks to two years to finish depending on the method you use, the outside temperature, the types of materials in the pile, and how often you turned and watered the mixture. Typically, a home bin with

some moderate attention will finish a batch in three to six months, whereas a pile of ignored dead leaves will take a year or more.

Use your senses to decide when your compost is ready to use. First, it should look like the best dark crumbly garden soil you've ever seen. The original materials should all be unrecognizable except for a few hard-to-break-down odds and ends like cherry pits, corncobs, and nutshells (these can be picked or screened out if they bother you). You may also notice streaks or areas of your pile covered with white powder especially if it reached maximum heat. These are simply large concentrations of composting microbes and are a sign of healthy, vital compost.

The compost should smell like the forest floor after a spring rain—sweet, fresh, and earthy. If it smells rotten or moldy, it's not done yet or you may need to do some troubleshooting (see Chapter 9). Also, feel the interior of the pile. If the temperature inside is significantly higher than the temperature outside, the pile is still decaying and the compost isn't ready.

When to Apply Compost

If you're in a hurry, you can add unfinished compost directly to your garden beds. However, it might tie up some of the available nitrogen in the soil, leaving your plants a little hungry. Unfinished compost can also retard the germination of some seeds, although a few plants like corn and squash actually seem to thrive on it. If you do use half-finished compost, apply it in the fall so that it can finish rotting in the ground by springtime and be available to feed all your green friends.

The best time to apply compost to your soil is two to four weeks before you plant. This gives

the compost time to get integrated and stabilized within the soil. If you use compost as a mulch, apply it a few weeks before or after you've planted seeds so that they'll have time to germinate properly.

Finished compost left standing in an exposed pile for weeks will begin to lose its nutrients into the ground through leaching. If you want to keep your compost as nutritious as possible, cover the finished pile with a tarp until you need it.

HOW MUCH COMPOST WILL I HAVE?

As a rule of thumb, your finished compost will shrink down to about half the volume of the raw materials you started with. For instance, one cubic yard of ingredients (3 by 3 by 3 feet—considered the minimum size for a pile) will finish as about one-half a cubic yard of compost. But what we lose in volume, we make up in density—that finished compost will weigh almost 500 pounds! And that's enough to cover a 150-square-foot garden with a 1-inch layer of compost.

Using Compost in the Garden

Growing plants love compost. Annual and perennial flowers, herbs, vegetables, and berry bushes will all benefit from regular applications of well-finished brown gold. For established garden beds, all you need to do is spread about one-half inch of compost per year to reap a maximum benefit. Of course, you can add more—lots of compost will not burn the tender roots of young plants like large doses of commercial synthetic fertilizer will. Simply spread the compost and rake, till, or shovel it in.

You can give your new garden beds a healthy head start by adding 1 to 2 inches of finished compost and then working it in with a tiller or a shovel to a depth of 4 to 6 inches. By incorporating it in deeper, you make the nutrients available to future roots and you help your soil retain moisture during long dry spells.

Some plants, like tomatoes, corn, and roses, are heavier feeders and will benefit from additional amounts of compost worked into the soil or added as a side dressing during the summer. Gardeners in warmer climates may also find that they need more compost because their growing season is longer and their plants live longer and require more nutrients. Crops growing in rainy climates and sandy soils also benefit from additional amounts of compost to replenish the nutrients that are constantly leached away.

Using Compost on Your Lawn

There lives a great myth in this country that the only way to have a gorgeous, lush, emerald-green lawn is to apply frequent doses of harsh fertilizers, dangerous herbicides, and polluting pesticides. Tons and tons of these chemicals are dumped every year on suburban lawns just to keep them looking good and green. And more and more often we hear how these sprays and powders harm the health of our children and pets and pollute our groundwater.

There is a better way, of course, and it begins and ends with compost. Adding compost to a new or established lawn will keep it well fed and able to retain water during dry spells. The compost feeds and invigorates the soil, which in turn builds a stronger, healthier turf that's better able to resist all kinds of diseases and pests. Compost treatments are nontoxic and cheap, and they save millions of gallons of water every year. What more can anyone ask for?

For newly established lawns, incorporate as much compost as possible into the soil before you lay your sod or scatter your grass seed. And when patching, work a few shovelfuls into those bare spots before reseeding. To fertilize an existing lawn, spread some coarsely screened compost across the yard. Use a lawn rake to spread it evenly. Don't worry about suffocating the grass—as long as you don't entirely bury the green shoots, the compost will all disappear in a few days.

If your lawn is sickly and needs a deeper, quicker treatment, use a garden fork or toothed aerator to poke some holes in your sod before you add the compost. A standard garden fork works well for small lawns, and you can rent special toothed lawn aerators for larger expanses. These gas-powered aerators look like oversize walk-behind mowers and pull out plugs of turf to allow the compost to get to the roots quicker.

And don't forget that adding compost over the years has a cumulative effect on the soil. The organic matter will stay there for many years to come, keeping the soil rich and friable—unlike the one-shot chemical treatments.

Using Compost for Trees and Shrubs

All established trees and shrubs benefit from a compost treatment. The best way to give your tall friends a treat is to work some finished compost into the soil under the tree branches. This area—from the trunk to the ends of the branches—is known as the drip ring. Compost added here will eventually reach the roots and promote healthy growth. If the roots are near the surface, don't risk injuring them by working in the compost. Spread it around as a top dressing—it will still reach the deeper roots, although it may take a little longer. You can give sickly trees and shrubs a faster-acting treatment by digging a few holes in the drip ring and then filling them with compost. And don't forget the healthy benefits of regular applications of compost tea also (see box on page 122).

You can also get new trees or shrubs off to a good start by adding a few shovelfuls of compost to the planting hole along with a healthy amount of peat moss. The peat helps keep the soil loose, and the compost will feed the new roots. Don't add too much compost, though. The roots might get too happy where they are and not extend out as they should.

Using Compost for Houseplants and Container Plants

Because containerized plants are so dependent on the small amount of material that surrounds their roots, they need a special blend of soils to stay healthy. For a perfect homemade potting soil, mix equal amounts of sifted compost, sand, and good garden soil. You can also buy bagged potting soil mixes but beware—although many of them are of high quality, others are not, and a bad potting soil can harden like cement after a short while. Look for mixes that list their ingredients on the package.

When it's time to feed your jade plants and sansevieria, spare them the green chemical brew and sprinkle a little finished compost on top of the soil instead. Compost tea (see box on page 122) is also an ideal beverage to serve to all your potted pals. They'll thank you for years to come.

Using Compost as a Mulch

Mulch is any material used to cover the soil around an established plant. Mulches can be organic (grass clippings, pine-bark nuggets, or seaweed) or inorganic (plastic sheets or old pieces of carpet). Mulching benefits plants in several ways: it helps the soil retain moisture, it smothers weeds, and it protects young roots.

Using compost as a mulch goes several steps further. Finished compost feeds your plants and even protects them from disease organisms. Here's an interesting fact about compost: the way you apply it determines the way it affects your plants. While compost dug in deep will improve the fertility and texture of the soil, a thin mulch of compost has been found to be the best way to prevent disease from harming your plants.

Spread your compost mulch around trees, shrubs, seedlings, and bushes. Thicker layers are more effective at suppressing weeds and keeping the soil moist. If you use compost as a mulch around young seedlings, make sure it's finished decomposing. Unfinished compost can tie up soil nitrogen and rob the young plants of nutrients.

Using Compost to Start Seeds and Transplants

Finished compost from a super-hot pile can be an ideal medium in which to start seeds. However, since casually made piles don't often get hot enough, weed seeds and plant pathogens may not be destroyed. If they linger, the diseases can affect your tender young seedlings. Also, unless you're a very sharp-sighted gardener, you may mistake some sprouted dandelion weeds for your Big Boy tomatoes. One solution is to sterilize the compost (or any soil you use to start seeds) in an oven, but that process kills off all the microbes, good and bad, and creates a most unpleasant smell in your kitchen.

So unless you're sure that your compost pile went thermophilic (reached 160°F.), it's probably not wise to use compost to start seeds. Use a special seed-starting mix instead. But once the seedlings are ready to be transplanted, any weeds or diseases that may exist in your compost won't threaten the young plants as much. Don't hesitate to add finished compost to the bigger pot or the soil when the plants are ready to go outdoors.

A SPOT OF TEA?

One of the best ways to make all your plants healthy and happy is to serve them a cup or two of compost tea. Here's how to make this easy-to-use elixir. Toss a few shovelfuls of finished compost into a bucket or small barrel of water, stir, and let brew for a day or two until the water turns amber in color and the solids have settled to the bottom. Siphon, pour off or ladle out the brown liquid and use it to water all your indoor and outdoor plants. You can even put some in a pump sprayer and spray the plants' leaves to deliver them a nutritious meal (this is known as foliar feeding). Using compost tea is also an excellent way to inoculate your next pile: just sprinkle some on as you build your compost pile and you'll be adding lots of the tiny microbes that are best adapted to your backyard.

If you really like tea parties, you can make a giant tea bag using an old pillowcase or burlap sack. Fill it with compost, tie or knot the top, and place it in a small barrel of water. That way you won't have to siphon or pour off the finished tea—you can simply remove the tea bag. You can also make smaller amounts using an old sock in a watering can. Let the tea brew for a few days before offering it to your garden plants. If you want to, you can even install a spigot at the bottom of the bucket or barrel to fill your watering can.

The same compost can be used to make tea several times before it begins to lose its potency. Even then it will have value, though, so spread the spent compost on your garden or toss it back into the pile.

MAKING A COMPOST SCREEN

You don't have to sift your compost for most purposes. But if you want to include a more powdery compost in your potting soil mix or spread it on your lawn, you may want to shake it through a screen.

You can make a simple compost screen out of pieces of old wood and some hardware screen. Make a simple wooden frame to whatever dimensions you want. It can be small enough to shake with one hand or large enough to sit on top of a garden cart. Buy 1/2-inch screening for coarse uses or a 1/4-inch screen for finer applications. With a staple gun, attach the screen to the bottom of the frame. Cover any sharp screen edges with duct tape or bend them in such a way to keep your hands from getting cut.

With a large-frame screen, you can process your compost by the shovelful. Simply place the frame atop a wheelbarrow or cart, then shovel and shake. Smaller frames take longer, naturally. What do you do with all the big chunky pieces? Give them another ride in the pile. And if you don't need much screened compost, consider using an old kitchen colander. You can also buy compost screens through many of the sources listed in the "Accessories" chapter.

GETTING A FEEL FOR YOUR SOIL

An easy way to test the health of your soil is to grab a handful and give it a squeeze. If it compresses into a sticky lump of clay, you're going to need a lot of compost to help break up and loosen your soil. If the squeezed handful falls apart into a sandy mess, you will need lots of compost to help your soil retain water. Good healthy garden soil should hold together loosely when squeezed and not feel too sticky or gritty. Even so, adding compost will make a good soil even better.

TROUBLESHOOTING

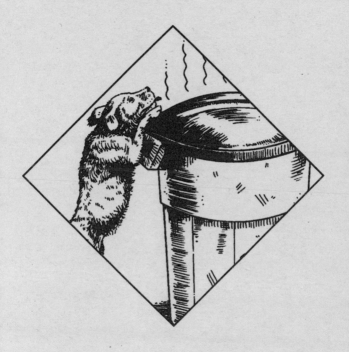

*C*OMPOSTING IS A SCIENCE, BUT IT'S CER-
tainly not brain surgery. Once you
understand the few basic principles,
making compost is an almost foolproof process
that anyone can master. However, there are piles
out there that just won't behave. They may
become unruly or stubborn; they might even
begin to attract some unwanted visitors. Don't
take these problems personally—bad piles
sometimes do happen to good people. Just find
your problem here and get your bin back on
track.

Rodents

Eeek!! There's a mouse in the compost! That's all
it would take to shut down most backyard composting in this country. If mice, squirrels, and
other long-toothed furry things show up in your

heap, don't sweat yet. First, make sure you have an active compost pile; a slowly decaying heap often becomes both restaurant and hotel to pests. Get your pile stimulated with some extra nitrogen and make sure there's enough water to keep the composting microbes happy. Once the pile begins to heat up, these squatters should move along.

If they don't go away, reduce the number of kitchen scraps you toss into your bin. These tasty morsels may be attracting your visitors. And when you do add scraps, keep them toward the center of the pile and see that they're covered with grass, leaves, or other yard waste. Also make sure that you and others in your family are not putting any meat, fat, cheese, or oil into the pile. These compost no-no's are sure to attract every furry creature for miles.

If the problem persists, you may have to make or buy a rodent-resistant bin. You can make one out of sturdy wood, thick plastic, or even sheet metal. Many gardeners use a heavy gnaw-resistant wire mesh ($1/4$-to-$1/2$ inches of 16-to-20-gauge) to allow adequate air circulation. Keeping the bin on a concrete slab or on patio stones will also frustrate burrowing rodents. Skunks and raccoons are often strong or smart enough to remove the lid from a bin in order to dine out. So find a bin with a tight lid or secure the lid with a bungee cord or a heavy rock.

Flies and Bugs

Your compost pile is full of life, and most of its residents are working hard to produce buckets of beautiful compost for you. Earthworms, sow bugs, slugs, and beetles all play a role in the decomposition process and should not be any bother. A few types of insects, however, can become a nuisance.

Fruit flies love to feed and breed in fruit and vegetable scraps on the top of your pile, and a small cloud of them may rise up to greet you every time you lift the lid from your bin. Although fruit flies are not a health problem, they can be vexatious. Control them by covering all your additions of kitchen scraps with some soil, ground leaves, peat moss, or sawdust. Soil gnats can be controlled in a similar way. Larger flies, like houseflies and horseflies, don't usually bother with compost piles unless you've made the mistake of adding meat or fish scraps.

Everybody's least favorite guest, the cockroach, may also show up in your pile, especially if you live in a warm climate. In the North, roaches usually stay indoors where the pickings are better, but if they become bothersome, cut back on kitchen scraps or stop adding them to the heap. You can also spread diatomaceous earth around the base of the pile to discourage their raids. This fine powdery substance is the skeletal remains of fossilized diatoms. It is also used to ward off slugs in the garden. Although it's nontoxic, you should follow package directions and wear a dust mask and gloves when you apply it.

Unpleasant smells

A healthy, working compost pile is not odor-free. It should have a rich, earthy aroma while it cooks and a forest-floor fragrance when it's done. If your pile develops sewer breath instead, then something is out of balance. In most cases, off odors are caused by a buildup of anaerobic bacteria. These decomposers show up when their hardworking cousins, the aerobic bacteria, have either drowned or suffocated. And not only do they have halitosis but they work at a much slower pace.

Give these smelly slouches the heave-ho by

getting your pile breathing again. Start by turning, stirring, poking, or fluffing to bring more oxygen into the pile. Break up any parts that have become dense and compacted. If your pile has become too wet and your aerobic friends have drowned, resuscitate them by mixing in some dry material like straw, sawdust, or shredded newspaper. You can also spread the pile out a bit on a dry day if that's convenient. Powdered lime can be sprinkled on a stinky pile, but it's only a temporary solution, like a mouthwash. It will also reduce the nitrogen content and may even change the pH of your finished compost.

An ammonia odor is a symptom of a different problem. This sharp smell indicates a pile that has too many nitrogen-heavy ingredients such as grass clippings or kitchen scraps. Turning the pile will help release the gaseous ammonia, but it won't prevent the problem from happening again. Correct this problem by mixing in some high carbon (brown) materials like straw or leaves.

Inactive Pile

Some piles just don't seem to decay. They sit there cold and lonely while their owners scratch their heads. They will eventually decompose and produce perfectly fine compost in several years, but you may not want to wait that long. If your pile hasn't ignited at all, there are a number of possible causes.

First, check the balance of ingredients. Have you built your pile with too many carbonaceous (brown) materials? If so, you need to incorporate more juicy nitrogen-rich substances such as grass clippings, manure, or kitchen scraps into the mix. A sprinkling of blood meal or a commercial compost inoculator can also jump-start a lazy heap.

Another cause of inactivity may be a lack or surplus of moisture. A pile that is bone-dry will mummify rather than rot, and a sopping wet pile will look and smell unattractive. Rejuvenate a dry pile with a thorough sprinkling, and cover or add dry ingredients to an overwet heap to get your rotting back on track.

If your compost pile is not big enough, it will lack the critical mass to really start cranking, and any heat that is generated by microbial activity will be lost to the air. Make sure your pile is at least a cubic yard (3 by 3 by 3 feet) in size to keep your biodegrading bugs toasty.

All compost piles slow down in the colder months. Sometimes they even stop when the thermometer drops below freezing. You can create a bigger or better-insulated pile if you want to keep the process active all winter, but there's no harm in just waiting for the spring thaw and the return of microbial activity.

ACCESSORIES

COMPOST MAKING IS SURELY A MINIMAL-ist's delight. You really don't need any-thing more than a few raw ingredients, a place to pile them, and some patience. But the rest of us like to have a few tools and machines to make the pile rot a little quicker. Here's a list of items that can help you compost more effectively:

Forks

When it comes time to turn the pile, most people reach for a forked garden tool of one kind or another. Traditional garden forks have flat, thick tines and short handles and are designed primar-ily for loosening the soil in garden beds. They can be used to turn compost in a pinch, but they're probably not the best tool for the job. The long handle and needle-sharp tines of a tra-ditional pitchfork are better suited for turning a heap, especially if the pile contains large amounts of dry, fluffy material, like leaves or straw. But if you plan on actively turning or mixing your compost every few weeks, spend a few extra dollars and get yourself a special compost fork or manure fork. These tools look much like pitchforks but have more tines (up to seven) and a spoonlike shape that allows you to pick up and move rotting material with ease.

Whichever fork you choose, make sure the steel has been tempered and that the head is riveted rather than glued onto the handle. If you are buying a new short-handled garden fork, make sure you get one with a *D*-shaped handle to give you extra leverage and a better grip. And if you decide to leave a fork permanently parked by your pile, find one with a fiberglass handle that won't rot in the elements.

Aerating Tools

If you have a passive, unturned pile that is rather difficult to stir or turn with a pitchfork, consider buying a compost aerating tool. These simple yet clever devices are designed to poke holes in your pile to allow greater air flow, which helps speed up the decomposition and reduce any possible odors. The most commonly available type has a pointy head with two small hinged wings that open up as you pull the tool out. With this tool, you can actually do a fair job of mixing the ingredients while aerating at the same time. Other aerating tools look and work like giant corkscrews or are simply oversized bits that you attach to your electric drill.

Thermometers

Most compost thermometers have a dial face and a long metal stem, up to 2 feet in length, and are used to monitor the interior temperature of an active pile. Although not necessary for most gardeners, they can be helpful in determining if your pile is reaching a thermophilic stage (160–170°F.) at which weed seeds and plant disease spores will be destroyed. Other compost thermometers consist of a probe attached by a long wire to a digital readout. With these instruments, you can monitor the pile's temperature from a distance or even from indoors.

Chipper-Shredders

Chipper-shredders are essentially garden-garbage disposal devices, which appeal to gardeners who like the idea of recycling all of their yard waste. Powered by electric motors or gas engines, these devices contain rotating blades and/or hammers that can shred leaves into a fine dust and turn branches into useful wood chips—both ideal ingredients for your compost pile. Small chipper-shredders can handle branches up to $1/2$ an inch in diameter, while larger ones can chew 3-inch-thick branches without groaning. Large units are expensive, however, and may be difficult to move around the yard. It's best to park one in a corner where all your chipping and shredding can be done and cover it with a tarp when it's not in use.

All newer chipper-shredders have well-designed safety features to prevent accidents. Still, as with all power tools, you should take precautions by wearing goggles, ear protection, long pants, thick gloves, and hard shoes when operating this tool. Also, don't wear any loose clothing, and if you have long hair, keep it tied back. Never try to dislodge a clog without first unplugging the electrical cord or disconnecting the spark plug wire.

Grinding up old tree branches, leaves, garden waste, and even kitchen scraps can be a lot of fun—you might even get your teenage son to help out with this chore. Plus you get a clean yard along with your big pile of instant compost ingredients. When shredding, try to avoid too many wet, dirty leaves. These tend to clog the machine and will dull the blades prematurely. To check blade sharpness, see if the unit will feed itself a branch dropped into the hopper. If you have to push down on the branch to get it chipped, it's time to sharpen.

You can also call your conventional lawnmower into duty to shred old garden plants and piles of leaves. Simply spread the materials to be shredded on a patch of lawn, set the mower's deck to medium-high, and make a few passes over the debris. If you've got a side-bagging mower, it's now full of wonderfully shredded stuff—perfect for compost. If there's no bag, you can rake up the ground-up plant matter or just leave it on the lawn to decompose. As always, wear protective clothing and be careful of flying debris.

Leaf Shredders

If you've got a lot of shade trees, you've got a lot of fall leaves. Dead leaves are good compost ingredients, but shredded leaves are much better—they decay quicker and take up less space. Consider purchasing a specially designed leaf shredder to help you process your leafy abundance. These are usually lightweight electric machines that are very effective and yet not nearly as expensive as a chipper-shredder. You just feed handfuls of dried leaves into the mouth of these self-standing units and the shredded matter falls out the bottom. They can be easily adjusted for either fine or coarse shredding.

If you already have an electric- or gas-powered leaf blower, check the manual to see if it can be used as a leaf sucker and shredder also. Most newer units can be reversed and used to vacuum leaves, shred them, and deposit them in a cloth bag that hangs over your shoulder. They are dandy for cleaning up the corners of your yard where leaves like to collect. The blowers with metal rather than plastic blades give a finer shred and will clog less.

Some innovative gardeners have drafted their old conventional string trimmers (weed whackers) to shred their piles of autumn leaves. They just dump their dried leaves into a barrel, drum, or other container, insert the string trimmer, and start to shred—just like turning on the blender!

COMPOSTING
WITH WORMS

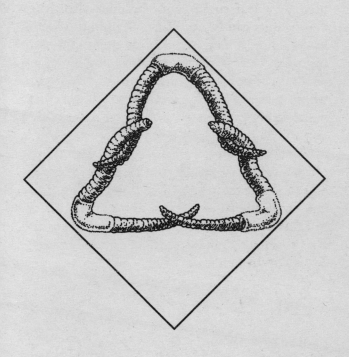

*L*ET'S SAY YOU REALLY LIKE THIS IDEA OF composting, but there you are, living in the Metropolis Apartment Building, twenty-six floors above the earth. You certainly don't have any yard waste to dispose of, but you would really like to recycle all those kitchen scraps you wind up tossing down the trash chute every week. Or perhaps you live in the country but your compost bin is located way out in the back forty and not easy to reach when there's snow and ice on the ground. You still want to dispose of your winter wastes in an ecologically responsible fashion. The answer to both situations is worms or, more specifically, composting with worms. And all you need is a small box, some simple bedding material, and a pound or two of hungry earthworms. In no time you'll have a new way to compost, your kids will be fascinated, and you'll be the talk of your neighborhood!

Why Use Worms?

Aristotle once called earthworms the "intestines of the earth," and it's easy to see why. They eat all kinds of organic matter, mix it up with microbes in their guts, and excrete it as nutrient-rich matter. Worm droppings, or castings, are highly valued by gardeners as one of the finest plant foods and soil conditioners available. All earthworms are eager eaters, but red worms are especially well suited to life indoors.

You can set up a little two- by three-foot worm box almost anywhere—on a balcony, under a bed, or next to the washer—and feed your wrigglers all the kitchen scraps your family produces. Once in their box, your polite little guests will eagerly eat your garbage day after day. They are shy by nature and love the dark, so you won't have to worry about them escaping. In fact, they may become favorite pets—they're quiet and clean, and they don't mind if you take off for a few weeks.

A Home for Your Worms

A worm bin need not be anything fancy or complicated. Because red worms feed near the surface, the box should be no more than one foot deep. Shallow boxes also keep the bedding from becoming too compressed. The box should have

holes drilled in the bottom and be elevated a few inches to allow for good air circulation. As in normal composting, you want to avoid anaerobic (no oxygen) conditions for best results. A 1- by 2- by 3-foot box will accommodate about 6 pounds of scraps a week from a family of four. You can build a box from pieces of scrap wood, but be sure to avoid cedar, redwood, and any pressure-treated lumber, all of which can be unhealthy for your wriggler population. You can also use an old plastic bin or metal washtub as long as it has never held harsh chemicals. All containers should have a number of finger-size holes drilled in the sides and bottom for additional air flow and to allow any excess water to drain off. (Don't fret; the worms won't escape.) With blocks of wood, raise the bin up an inch or so for maximum air circulation, and keep a tray, mat, or newspaper underneath to catch any excess moisture or worm castings that may fall out.

Of course, you can make a more elaborate worm bin. Add casters, a seat back, and a cushion and you've got patio furniture. Build one on cabinet rollers to pull out of a low cupboard in your kitchen. Add Grateful Dead decals or stencil the bin to match your wallpaper. Of course, manufactured bins are also available.

Location, Location, Location

Red worms are adaptable little fellows, but they do need a few basics to survive. Their box shouldn't be placed in any part of the home or yard that gets too warm (85°F. or higher), so avoid your hot attic, outdoor areas in full sun, and your summer greenhouse. Worms will also perish in freezing temperatures, so if your box is outdoors, you must bring it indoors, or at least protect it with insulating layers of straw or leaves, during the colder months. Don't disturb the worms by adding food during very cold

BUILDING A WORM BIN

You can construct a sturdy wooden bin from a 4- by 4-foot sheet of $1/2$-inch exterior-grade plywood and a few galvanized screws or nails. With a table saw or circular saw, cut four side pieces $23^1/2$ inches long by 12 inches wide. Nail or screw these together to form a square box. Cut another piece 24 by 24 inches square for the bottom, and attach it with nails or screws. Drill about fifteen $1/2$-inch holes in the bottom to allow for better air circulation and occasional draining. Paint the bin inside and out with a nontoxic wood preservative such as polyurethane or a good exterior paint and let it dry thoroughly. You can make a similarly designed 1- by 2- by 3-foot box from a larger sheet of plywood.

weather—the box may lose heat quickly and the worms can perish.

Like all living creatures, worms need moisture and good ventilation. They respire through their skin, and they must stay in a moist medium. An occasional sprinkling of water may be needed, but be aware that they're not aquatic animals and they'll drown in an overwatered, soggy bin.

Because they take in oxygen and release carbon dioxide, adequate air circulation is important. That's why worm bins are shallow and have holes in the bottom and sides.

So where do you put your worm box? The kitchen is ideal, as it's the source of all the food scraps, but for heaven's sake, don't tell your dinner guests. A patio site is great, especially when you need to do the messy job of separating out the castings, but make sure they don't bake or freeze. A bin in an airy garage will certainly be out of your way (as long as the worms don't freeze), as will a box in a basement, but both sites may be too far from the kitchen for the cook to take those few extra steps.

Wherever you situate your bin, don't let your cats use it as an additional litter box. That would be unhealthy for your worms and possibly for you as well. Cat droppings may contain cysts of a parasitic disease organism that can affect humans—especially developing fetuses. If you have cats, make sure your worm box has a sturdy lid. This should keep out nosy dogs, too.

Bedding Materials

Worms need a bedding material in which to live and reproduce, and this medium needs to be organic and edible, as the worms consume their bedding along with their table scraps. The bedding also must be able to hold moisture and light

enough so it won't compact and stop air from circulating.

Most people use a paper product for bedding. Shredded cardboard is clean and odor free, but it might be hard to find. You can shred it yourself if you have the patience. Shredded bond paper is clean, dust free, and available at many offices, but it doesn't hold moisture as well. Newspaper, which is cheap and easy to find, is probably the most popular bedding material used in worm boxes. Tear sheets into strips 2 to 4 inches wide for best results.

Paper beddings must be moistened thoroughly and then squeezed out before filling the bin. It's also a good idea to toss in a handful of garden soil to provide the worms with a little grit to help their digestion. All bedding will eventually turn into castings, so remember to add fresh bedding before the old material is completely exhausted.

The Right Worms to Use

Red worms (*Eisenia foetida*) are the only real choice for worm boxes. They eat large quantities, do well in confinement, and can take the warmer environment found in most homes. Known also as red wigglers and red hybrids, these 3- to 4-inch long worms are native to North America and might easily be found in a pile of compost or leaf mold sitting in your backyard. They're also sold in bait shops and can be mail-ordered through companies listed in the back of fishing and gardening magazines. Don't try to use regular earthworms, or night crawlers, as some people call them. These bigger critters are much more temperature-sensitive and don't do well in captivity.

How many worms do you need? Try to estimate how many pounds of scraps your kitchen produces each day. For every pound of waste, you should have about 2 pounds of worms. Red worms are usually sold by the pound, and they can be mail-ordered year-round. There are about 1,000 worms per pound, so don't bother assigning pet names to your wigglers. Don't worry too much about having too many or too few worms—their numbers will stabilize in a short while. If there are too few, they will breed according to how much food they have. If you have too many, they'll stop breeding and some may even die off.

Starting the Box

First, thoroughly soak the bedding material in a bucket of water until it's sopping wet. Add a few handfuls of good garden soil for a grit source and mix with the bedding. Pour the mixture into the bin and dump in the worms. They will naturally begin to go underground, especially if the light is bright. After a while, remove any dead ones left on the surface. Cover the box with a sheet of black plastic made from a trash bag or with a fitted lid, if you have one. This keeps the worms moist and happy in the dark. You can now start adding kitchen scraps.

Feeding Time

As with your big old compost pile out back, you can add just about any vegetable matter that comes from your kitchen. This includes apple cores, potato skins, carrot tops, fruit rinds, coffee

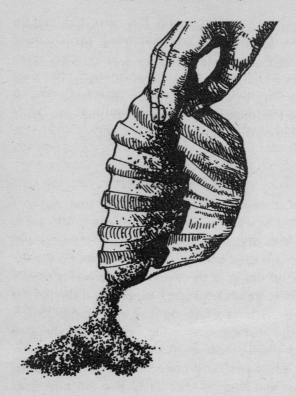

grounds (a wormy favorite) and paper filters, tea bags, lettuce leaves, and so on. You can also add spoiled foods and leftovers such as cooked cereal, moldy bread, and stale cake. And just as in your big pile, you can speed things up by chopping or grinding the scraps before dumping them in the box.

With some care, you can also add certain items that aren't recommended for outdoor compost piles such as old cheese and small amounts of meat and bones. However, they may start to smell bad and could attract vermin, so most people don't bother. Naturally, you shouldn't add any of the no-no's of any composting system: plastic, glass, rubber, metal, or pet waste. Garden waste is usually too voluminous and too dense for a small box; throw it into your big outdoor pile instead.

Feeding your worms is easy. Once you've collected a few cups of kitchen waste, remove the plastic sheet or lid and bury the scraps underneath some of the bedding. Change the location of each worm meal so that the waste is spread about the bedding. To keep track of where you've made a deposit, stick an old pencil or a piece of straw in the spot where you made the last one. By the time you've made the circuit around the box, the first deposit should be well on its way to compost.

Holiday seasons can produce a sudden glut of kitchen scraps, and if you add them all at once, you may overwhelm the worms. The food may begin to rot anaerobically, resulting in some nasty odors. Don't overload your worms with a Christmas or Thanksgiving dinner! Take the surplus to your outdoor pile, if you have one, or store it in a cold area and feed it to the box gradually.

Your worms can certainly stand a fast for a week or two without any damage, but they do eventually need food to thrive. Without it they'll turn into a population of small, undernourished worms, and if you totally neglect them, the whole colony may starve to death.

Worm Care

Aside from a few square meals, red worms need very little. No daily walks, no special vitamins, no trips to the vet. They're almost as carefree as a Pet Rock. You should, however, watch for signs that the box is drying out. If the bedding feels dry, sprinkle the surface with a little water.

After a few months, the bedding will turn dark and begin to look indistinguishable from the pelletlike castings. You'll also notice that the bedding level has dropped as both the food and bedding have been consumed and converted into castings. Now's the time to harvest some of that rich vermicompost and rejuvenate the box. If you don't change the bedding, the worms will eventually all die and decompose.

HARVESTING YOUR VERMICOMPOST

There are a number of ways to separate your worms from the finished vermicompost. One way is to open the bin and turn on the lights or take your bin out in the daylight. In a few minutes the bright light will have driven all the wrigglers to the bottom, and you can gently scoop some of the finished vermicompost off the surface. Wait a few more minutes for the worms to dive deeper and then scoop off the next layer. You will eventually get to a level where it's hard to remove compost without removing or hurting your worms, and that's the place to stop. Now dump the remainder of the bedding and worms onto a plastic sheet and fill the box with fresh bedding. Once the box is filled, shake the worms back into the box to begin again.

You can also dump everything out at once onto a tarp, separate it into smaller piles, and wait while the worms dig down. Scoop off the top of each pile and wait before scooping again. Again, stop at the level where the worms could be hurt and have nowhere to go. Fill the bin with new bedding and dump the worms back in,

Another method of harvesting vermicompost

is simply to push most of the bin's contents to one side and fill the space with fresh bedding. Add your kitchen scraps only on the new-bedding side. In a short while all the worms will be there and you can scoop out the old side with minimal damage.

Harvest time is a good time to share surplus worms with friends. Show your loved ones how much you care for them by handing them a pound or two of red worms—wrapped and tied with a bow, please. You can give away up to half of your population without slowing things down too much.

SPOTTING AND SOLVING PROBLEMS

You may have to make a few adjustments to your worm box if something gets out of balance. Here are the common problems you may encounter and ways to solve them.

FRUIT FLIES.   They like fruit, they like moisture, and they can have a party in your worm box. They arrive in the summer on fruit peels and rinds, but they're basically harmless—they don't bite and they don't carry diseases. They do swarm above a worm box in a small cloud, which may irritate you, so if they show up, here's how to give them the boot. First make sure you are burying your scraps under the bedding, not just letting them sit on top. If the flies persist, suck them up with the vacuum cleaner hose or just move the bin outside to a shady spot for the warm season and ignore their antics.

ODORS.   If the bin gets a bit smelly, you've probably overloaded it with food, which is rotting before the worms can consume it. Stop adding food and let the worms catch up. Odors can also be caused by a bin that is too wet. Check the bottom for wetness and fluff up the bedding or add some fresh newspaper to absorb the excess moisture. Drill more holes in the bottom of the bin if this occurs frequently.

DRIPPING BIN.   If you add mostly wet kitchen scraps and your box is in a humid area, you may get a little moisture seeping from the bottom. If this persists, remove the lid or plastic sheet and allow the box to dry out a bit. Use a sheet of newspaper instead of the lid, or just leave the bin uncovered—but don't let the cat start using it for a litter box!

DEAD WORMS.   Worms will perish if the bin becomes too hot or too cold, too wet or too dry, or if all the bedding has been consumed. Correct these conditions and replenish your worm population if necessary.

SEX SECRETS OF THE RASCALLY REDWORM

Red worms, like earthworms, are hermaphroditic—they contain both male and female organs. They reach sexual maturity four to six weeks after birth and begin to develop a thickened band, or clitellum, around their middle. When they mate, two worms join together at the clitellum and exchange sperm, which they hold in sperm storage sacs. Later, a cocoon forms over each worm's clitellum. As the cocoon is shed, it passes over the ovaries and storage sacs and collects the eggs and sperm. Once this grain-of-rice-size cocoon is shed, it closes up at both ends and fertilization occurs within. Several weeks later two or three baby worms hatch out. Red worms can produce over four hundred offspring a year.

USING VERMICOMPOST

Worm castings, or vermicompost, is considered one of the finest soil amendments and plant foods available. Use as much as you want in potting soils and garden beds. Sprinkle a little on the soil in your potted plants to give them a deep, slow feeding. Add a scoop to your watering can and let it steep for a few hours to make a worm tea with which to treat your floral friends.

You'll find lots of uses for this excellent fertilizer, as you will for all your compost.